MIDDLE SCHOOL
DOG'S BEST FRIEND

THE MIDDLE SCHOOL SERIES

THE WORST YEARS OF MY LIFE
(with Chris Tebbetts)
This is the insane story of my first year at middle school, when I, Rafe Khatchadorian, took on a real-life bear (sort of), sold my soul to the school bully, and fell for the most popular girl in school. Come join me, if you dare...

GET ME OUT OF HERE!
(with Chris Tebbetts)
We've moved to the big city, where I'm going to a super-fancy art school. The first project is to create something based on our exciting lives. But I have a BIG problem: my life is TOTALLY BORING. It's time for Operation Get a Life.

MY BROTHER IS A BIG, FAT LIAR
(with Lisa Papademetriou)
So you've heard all about my big brother, Rafe, and now it's time to set the record straight. I'm NOTHING like my brother. (Almost) EVERYTHING he says is a Big Fat Lie. And my book is 100 times better than Rafe's. I'm Georgia, and it's time for some payback... Khatchadorian style.

HOW I SURVIVED BULLIES, BROCCOLI, AND SNAKE HILL
(with Chris Tebbetts)

I'm excited for a fun summer at camp—until I find out it's
a summer *school* camp. There's no fun and games here,
I have a bunk mate called Booger Eater (it's pretty self-
explanatory), and we're up against the kids from the "Cool
Cabin"... there's gonna be a whole lotta trouble!

ULTIMATE SHOWDOWN
(with Julia Bergen)

Who would have thought that we—Rafe and Georgia—
would ever agree on anything? That's right—we're writing
a book together. Discover: Who has the best advice on
BULLIES? Who's got all the right DANCE MOVES? Who's
the cleverest Khatchadorian in town? And the best part?
We want you to be part of the fun too!

SAVE RAFE!
(with Chris Tebbetts)

I'm in worse trouble than ever! I need to survive a
gut-bustingly impossible outdoor excursion so I can return
to school next year. Watch me as I become "buddies" with
the scariest girl on the planet, raft down the rapids on a
deadly river, and ultimately learn the most
important lesson of my life.

JUST MY ROTTEN LUCK
(with Chris Tebbetts)

I'm heading back to the place it all began: Hills Village
Middle School, but only if I take "special" classes... If that
wasn't bad enough, when I somehow land a place on the
school football team, I find myself playing alongside none
other than the biggest bully in school, Miller the Killer!

Also by James Patterson

I Funny series
I Funny (*with Chris Grabenstein*)
I Even Funnier (*with Chris Grabenstein*)
I Totally Funniest (*with Chris Grabenstein*)
I Funny TV (*with Chris Grabenstein*)

Treasure Hunters series
Treasure Hunters (*with Chris Grabenstein*)
Danger Down the Nile (*with Chris Grabenstein*)
Secret of the Forbidden City (*with Chris Grabenstein*)
Peril at the Top of the World (*with Chris Grabenstein*)

House of Robots series
House of Robots (*with Chris Grabenstein*)
Robots Go Wild! (*with Chris Grabenstein*)

Other illustrated novels
Kenny Wright: Superhero (*with Chris Grabenstein*)
Jacky Ha-Ha (*with Chris Grabenstein*)

Daniel X series
The Dangerous Days of Daniel X (*with Michael Ledwidge*)
Watch the Skies (*with Ned Rust*)
Demons and Druids (*with Adam Sadler*)
Game Over (*with Ned Rust*)
Armageddon (*with Chris Grabenstein*)
Lights Out (*with Chris Grabenstein*)

For more information about James Patterson's novels, visit
www.jamespatterson.co.uk

Or become a fan on Facebook

MIDDLE SCHOOL

DOG'S BEST FRIEND

JAMES PATTERSON

AND CHRIS TEBBETTS

ILLUSTRATED BY JOMIKE TEJIDO

1 3 5 7 9 10 8 6 4 2

Young Arrow
20 Vauxhall Bridge Road
London SW1V 2SA

Young Arrow is part of the Penguin Random House
group of companies whose addresses can be found at
global.penguinrandomhouse.com

Penguin
Random House
UK

First published by Young Arrow in 2016

www.penguin.co.uk

A CIP catalogue record for this book is available
from the British Library

Hardback ISBN 9781784753887
Trade paperback ISBN 9781784753894

Printed and bound by Clays Ltd, St Ives Plc

Penguin Random House is committed to a sustainable future
for our business, our readers and our planet. This book is made
from Forest Stewardship Council® certified paper.

MIX
Paper from
responsible sources
FSC
www.fsc.org   FSC® C018179

FOR ERiC, TRiSHA, EVELYNN,
ANN, BETH AND RYAN NAJORK
—J.P.

FOR LARRY JEAN
—C.T.

MIDDLE SCHOOL

DOG'S BEST FRIEND

LOOZER AND LEO IN:
Merry Christmas, LOOZER!
With special guest: Meatloaf!
Merry Christmas, Meatloaf!
Ruff!
Merry Christmas, Loozer!
A new pen! Just what I wanted!

CHAPTER 1

NOT-SO-MERRY CHRISTMAS

I slammed my sketchbook closed. Usually drawing comics made me feel better, but not today. It was Christmas morning, and even Loozer was having a better time than I was.

As for Leo, well...I can explain about him later.

I didn't exactly get a hoverboard and a ski trip under the tree that morning. Instead, I got some school clothes and two new books from Mom. Also a coupon from my sister, Georgia, for one turn unloading the dishwasher, and a "Christmas hug" from Grandma Dotty. Grandma said she was still working on her gifts.

The other thing I didn't get was a WormHole Premium Multi-Platform GameBox. That's what I *really* wanted, but I would have had a better chance asking Santa for the Empire State Building. Those WormHoles were *expensive*, and we weren't exactly rolling in dough that Christmas.

Still, I would have given my big toe for one of those systems. They could run games from all the other major brands, plus their own titles, which were the best ones out there, by far. That thing could practically clean your room and do your homework for you, it was *that* cool.

Not that I was obsessed or anything.

Well, okay, maybe a little bit.

But none of that was the *real* bummer.

"All right, I've got to get going," Mom said. It was only eleven in the morning, but she was putting on her coat to go to work. Yeah, that's right. On Christmas. The Madison Hotel was paying really good money for waitresses in their banquet hall that day, and Mom couldn't afford to say no.

"I'll make it up to you guys," she said. "I'm off all day tomorrow and we'll have a real Christmas dinner then."

What were we going to say? It's not like Mom

wanted to work on Christmas. She was just looking out for us. The least we could do was act like it was no big deal.

"That sounds awesome!" I said.

"It'll be like having two Christmases!" Grandma said.

"Yeah!" Georgia said. "No problem, Mom."

I think she actually bought it too. And we might have pulled it off, if I hadn't opened my big mouth one more time. See, I have this bad habit of taking things a little too far sometimes.

Or a lot too far.

"Don't worry about it, Mom," I said. "Who needs Christmas, anyway? Not us!"

Yeah, right. Like any kid who celebrates Christmas was going to say *that*.

That's when Mom stopped buttoning her coat. She gave me this weird smile and her eyes got kind of watery.

"I'll be right back," she said. "I, um…forgot my keys."

Then she went into the bathroom and closed the door behind her. (FYI, Mom doesn't keep her keys in the bathroom.) She'd been spending a lot of time in there ever since she and my Learning Skills teacher, Mr. Fanucci, decided to stop dating after a while. I'll admit it kind of skeeved me out that they were seeing each other, but I'd one thousand times rather see them kissing than to see my mom sad.

"Way to go, big mouth," Georgia said.

"But…" I said. "I didn't mean to—"

"Yeah, you never do, Rafe," she said. Even Grandma was looking at me like I'd just taken the world's cruddiest Christmas and managed to make it even cruddier.

Which I guess I had.

Leave it to me.

So basically, that was strike one. I'll tell you about strike two in a minute. But the point is, my little Christmas disaster was the beginning of everything else that happened that winter.

I'm talking about how I got in hot water with Mom, almost lost my best friend (the furry one), launched my very own business empire, survived the Great Dog War of January, and learned a little magic along the way.

Which may not be where you thought this was going, but it totally is.

Read on, my friend.

CHAPTER 2

DOWN THE WORMHOLE

Let me make one thing clear before I say anything else. I had a ton of stuff to be grateful for. Even a bonehead like me knew that.

1. I had the best mom this side of anywhere. And the best grandma too. And...well, I had a sister. (I'd say I was grateful for Georgia, but I don't want to lie.)

2. We had a warm, safe apartment to live in and enough food to eat. Not everybody does, right?

3. I had my supercool dog, Junior.

4. I also had my awesome best friend, Flip Savage, who's just as crazy, fast on his feet, and fun to hang out with as Junior.

5. Hold on to your socks, because FLIP GOT A WORMHOLE PREMIUM MULTI-PLATFORM

GAMEBOX FOR CHRISTMAS!

So I probably don't have to tell you where I planned on spending the rest of school vacation—right there in Flip's basement, playing House of Thor, and Driving on the Ceiling, and Schoolyard Zombies, and my very favorite (and Flip's favorite, and pretty much anyone in the universe who knows anything about the WormHole's favorite), TrollQuest.

Flash forward a couple of days, and there we are in Flip's basement...

...deep into our first quest...

...and running for our lives.

We're sprinting across an open field with woods on either side. I look left. I look right. All I can see are glowing yellow eyes staring back from the trees. Those are the spider people we were told to watch out for. I haven't had to fight any of them yet, and if I'm lucky, I won't have to.

What we really need to do is get to the river. Supposedly, Grindle the road merchant left us a couple of canoes there, but you never know who you can trust around here. We spent our last gold nuggets for those boats. If we don't get onto the

river—fast—those spider people are going to be eating us for breakfast, lunch, and dinner.

"Keep going! Straight ahead!" Flip yells. Except his name is Brix here. He calls himself that because his character is all muscle and strong as a brick wall. Get it?

My name's Stinker, but only because I entered it in wrong at the beginning. It was supposed to be *Stinger,* for my punching skills. But now I don't know how to fix it without resetting the whole quest.

Oh well. I've got bigger problems to deal with— like staying alive long enough to reach that river.

Meanwhile, Grindle is as good as his word. There are two birch bark canoes waiting for us when we get to the water's edge. But we've also got a whole cluster of yellow-eyed spider freaks streaming out of the shadows as fast as their hairy legs can carry them.

"Go!" I yell.

"I *am!*" Flip yells.

I reach my canoe first, shove it into the water, and jump in. Brix is right behind me. And right behind him—

WHIZZZZ!

—a wad of acid goes shooting past my head. I look back and the spider people have stopped on the shore. They can't swim, but they sure do know how to spit.

"Just paddle! Don't look back!" Flip yells.

"I'm trying!" I say, working the controller as hard as I can. But then—

WHIZZZ...SIZZLE!

I look again and there's a hole burning its way right through the bark of my canoe.

"I'm hit!" I yell.

Water's pouring in and I'm running out of

options. There's no way I can swim to safety. This river is stocked with electric razor fish—the kind that will turn a troll into fish food faster than you can say "game over."

"Jump into my boat!" Flip says. He tries to paddle toward me, but the current is pulling us apart. The longer I wait, the harder this is going to get.

So I give it a shot. I stand up. The canoe nearly tips over, but I manage to keep my balance. Then I make the world's most desperate leap, out of my sinking boat, through the air, and—

"FLIII-IIIIP?"

Flip's mom yelled down the stairs so loud, my hand slipped right off the jump button.

"Is Rafe there with you?" she said.

"I'm here, Mrs. Savage," I said. Flip tried to pause the game, but it was too late. Stinker was already in the water, and those electric razor fish were doing exactly what you'd expect.

"Mom!" Flip yelled. "You just killed Rafe!"

"Sorry about that, Rafe," Mrs. Savage said. "But your mother is looking for you, and she didn't sound too happy on the phone."

"What time is it?" I said.

"It's quarter to six," Mrs. Savage said.

"It's WHAT?" I said. I dropped my controller on the couch. "I gotta go!"

"Just five more minutes," Flip said.

"Can't," I said, and ran up the stairs like I still had acid-spitting spider freaks coming after me. Because now I was on a whole new mission. This one was called Operation: Get Home Before My Dog Poops on the Floor Because I Lost Track of Time...Again.

And I'll just tell you right now. It was not a successful mission.

MAD MOM

I'M SORRY, I'M SORRY, I'M SORRY, I'M SORRY, I'M SORRY!" I said, running into the house.

It was six o'clock exactly and I knew I was supposed to be back at three to walk Junior. But it was too late. Right there on the living room rug was...well, let's just call it the evidence of my failed mission.

Do you remember how sad Mom was in Chapter 2? Well, take all that sad and replace it with mad. Then add some more mad, and sprinkle a bunch of sick and tired over the whole thing. That's about how she seemed when I got there.

In other words, I'd blown it. AGAIN. I felt so guilty, I couldn't even look at Mom. Or Junior.

"I'm really sorry," I said again. "I'll clean this up."

"Yes, you will," Mom said. "Then you're going to take Junior for his walk. And *then* we're going to have a talk about this. I thought you were ready for the responsibility of having a dog, Rafe. But maybe I was wrong."

"What?" I said. I covered Junior's ears, just in case he could understand. "But he's part of the family!"

"Yeah!" Georgia said, coming in from the kitchen. "We can't get rid of him! *Please?*"

Of course, she'd been listening. Georgia's like an international spy without any of the cool parts and all the annoying little sister parts. But she loves Junior as much as I do.

Mom closed her eyes and shook her head. Then she sat down and took a deep breath.

"No, of course," she said. "I'm sorry. I didn't mean that. It's been a long couple of weeks."

Besides working Christmas, she'd been doing double shifts at Swifty's Diner, six days a week. That meant leaving at five in the morning and getting back at four in the afternoon. Meanwhile, I'd been sitting around Flip's basement, playing TrollQuest and not even taking care of my own dog.

I didn't say a word. I just nodded and went to clean up the mess, while Georgia stared at me like I'd won the award for World's Worst Dog Owner.

Sometimes I wish I was a programmable cyborg instead of a human. Then at least I could set my brain for things like DON'T FORGET TO WALK THE DOG. Or even better, ERASE GEORGIA FROM MEMORY BANKS.

In the meantime, I was stuck there with my regular human brain. So as soon as I could, I picked up Junior's leash and took him out for a nice long walk, to get as far from my sister as humanly possible.

Also to give Mom some cooling-off time.

Like maybe until spring.

CHAPTER 4

PARK AND BARK

The great thing about dogs is that they never stay mad. As soon as Junior figured out where we were headed, he was in the best mood ever. Seriously, we could all learn a few things from our dogs.

By the time we got to the gate at the dog park, Junior was practically choking himself trying to get off the leash. He loves that place the way I love drawing, pizza, and school vacation, combined.

"Make sure that gate is latched!" some lady yelled. They're really picky about keeping the gate closed at the dog park, which I guess I can understand. But some people could afford to calm down about it, if you ask me.

"Hey, Muffin! Junior's here!" someone else said.

I called this place the Park and Bark. I knew most of the dogs' names, but not the owners'. They were just Poncho Lady and Really Loud Girl and Big Beard. Stuff like that.

Marley Grote also came to this park with her dog sometimes. She's a girl from school who maybe kind of sort of possibly was my first kiss awhile back. I'm not really sure what happened, but we don't really talk much anymore. Maybe I was supposed to do something after we kissed, but I didn't know what, and she never told me. Every time I see her I get a little weirded out, but the good news is that she went on vacation with her family over the break. So I won't be running into her here.

Meanwhile, Junior was saying hi to Muffin, and Charlie, and Blanco, and Jed, and Dakota and everyone else. Then Super-Tall Guy threw a tennis ball and they all went after it like it was a live rabbit covered in gravy. Already, Junior was having a great time.

Not me. Now I was just standing there, staring into space and trying to figure out how to make things better for Mom. Help out so she didn't have to work so much and be so tired all the time. Maybe I could get a job? The real question was, what could a middle school screw-up like me actually do? It's not like anyone would pay me for playing TrollQuest or picking up Junior's poop.

"O...M...G, could it *be* any colder out here?" someone said behind me.

"I know, right?" someone else said.

I turned around, and it was Starbucks Lady talking to Candy Crush. One of them always had a giant coffee, and the other one never stopped playing that game on her phone, even when she was talking to people.

"The depressing thing is—ooh!" Candy Crush said, crushing some candy. "Winter's just getting started. It's going to be long time until—ohhhhh, nooo!" I guess she'd just lost her game.

Then I heard someone else.

"Please, I'm begging you, Daisy. Just go!"

I looked over and Nose Ring Guy's basset hound was turning around in a million circles, looking for the perfect pee spot.

Nose Ring Guy didn't look too happy to be there either. Just like Starbucks Lady, Candy

Crush, and me. In fact, it seemed like the only ones who were in a good mood at the dog park were the dogs.

And that's when something inside my head went—CLICK!

Or maybe more like—BOOM!

You know how some ideas come on slowly, like a pot of boiling water? Not this one. This was more like an explosion. In a dynamite factory. Inside my brain.

I was going to start a business. A *dog-walking* business. It was the perfect idea, for three reasons.

1. It was going to make Mom happy. This was going to show her I could be responsible *and* earn my own money.

2. It was going to make Junior happy. You can't forget to walk the dog when you have a dog-walking business, right?

And 3…can I get a drumroll, please? Because if I played it right, I was going to turn this idea into enough cash for a WormHole Premium Multi-Platform GameBox of my very own.

And that's what you call a win-win-win.

In other words—BOOM!

CHAPTER 5

THE MAN WITH THE PLAN

I was all over the Internet that night. And no, I don't mean I was famous. I mean I was looking up everything I needed to know to make this happen.

I saw a bunch of stuff about creating "formal business plans," which one site said was like drawing a "road map" to my "goals and objectives."

So I started off by making a map, even if it wasn't the kind they meant. This one was a drawing of our neighborhood, with everyone we knew who had a dog.

Then I spent some time thinking about the money part, which is my favorite topic. First, I looked up the price of a WormHole. It was $399 for the same system Flip had, and it came preloaded

with three games, including TrollQuest.

So here's what I figured. I'd put half of everything I made in the bank. I already had fifteen dollars and forty-two cents in my savings account, which meant I still had to raise three hundred and eighty-some for the WormHole.

Then I'd keep the other half of what I earned stashed in my room for everything else. That way I wouldn't have to ask Mom every time I needed a dollar, or two, or ten.

After I looked at a couple more websites, I decided I could charge five bucks a walk. I didn't know how many dogs I could do in a day, but even if it was just three, that would be fifteen bucks right there.

Then I pulled out my calculator and *really* started getting excited. Because fifteen bucks times seven was a hundred and five dollars a week. And a hundred and five times four was four hundred and twenty bucks a month.

In fact, I thought, why stop there? Did Steve Jobs know he was going to be a zillionaire when he started building computers? Probably not. Did Jay-Z know he was recording his first million-

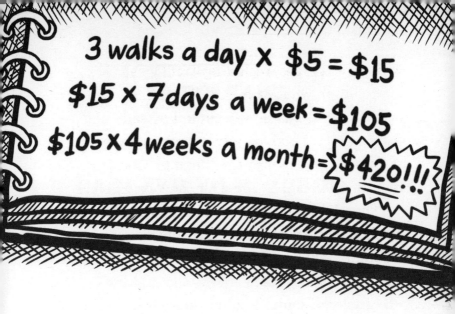

3 walks a day X $5 = $15
$15 × 7 days a week = $105
$105 × 4 weeks a month = $420!!!

selling platinum song when he made it? Probably not.

I'm not saying I was going to make a zillion bucks for sure. I'm just saying you can't buy a lottery ticket without thinking about winning, right? So you might as well think big.

And if you can manage that, you might as well think REALLY big.

In fact, I could just see it now...

CHAPTER 6

A MOGUL IN MY OWN MIND

There I am on my corporate jet, taking a bath in hundred-dollar bills while we zoom down to Miami for the weekend. We've got the opening of our one thousandth location coming up tomorrow, and it's our biggest one yet. Because what McDonald's is to hamburgers, that's what we're going to be to dog-walking.

This whole corporate empire thing is going way better than I ever could have imagined. Actually, scratch that. It's going *exactly* as well as I imagined. Good thing I remembered to think BIG.

So as soon as I finish covering myself in that new-money smell, I hop out of the tub and throw on one of those extra-fluffy robes. I'm late for a business meeting with my Corporate Vice-President.

And by *business meeting,* I mean the all-you-can-eat burger bar in the jet's executive dining room.

And by *Vice-President,* of course, I mean Junior.

"How are our earnings looking this quarter?" I ask, once we're sitting down to a couple of armadillo-size burgers.

Junior just gives me a paws-up, since his mouth is full. Not to mention, dogs can't talk. At least, not yet. We're still working on that bark-to-speech technology in the lab, but it's looking good for a summer rollout.

Meanwhile, I'm pretty sure huge corporations can have a whole ton of Vice-Presidents, so I'm cutting Flip in on this too. Junior is VP of Sales, Marketing, Kibble, and Treats.

And Flip is VP in Charge of All the Cool Stuff We Can Do Now That This Company Is Practically Made of Money.

Like for instance, opening the world's first life-size, interactive TrollQuest QuestPark we have planned.

And the tropical island I'm buying Mom for Mother's Day.

And the luxury ski condo for Grandma Dotty.

And maybe a nice pair of socks for Georgia.

Because you know what they say when you're thirty thousand feet up in your own private jet, with a mouthful of bacon-cheddar pizzaburger and nothing but profit on the horizon, right?

The sky's the limit, baby! Think big! Dream on!

And thank you for your business.

CHAPTER 7

FiRST CUSTOMER...iSH

When I got up the next morning, Mom was already long gone to work. Grandma was out playing mah-jongg at the senior center, and Georgia was doing homework. On vacation. Of course.

Now that we were both in middle school, we were allowed to be home alone for part of the daytime. So I was going to use that.

"I'm taking Junior for a walk," I said, and left out the rest. I didn't need Georgia knowing my business. At least, not until I actually had one.

And since I hadn't told Mom about it either, I stayed pretty close to home. For the time being, I was just going to talk to people we already knew. And the closest one of those on my map was Mr. Schneider, who lived around the corner.

Mr. Schneider was this really old guy who walked with a cane, even just to get the mail. He also had an old sheepdog named Max. I didn't know if Max needed much exercise, but it couldn't hurt to ask.

"Rafe!" Mr. Schneider said when he answered the door. "What can I do for you?"

"I was actually coming over to ask you about walking Max," I said.

"About what?" he said, putting a wrinkly hand up to his ear.

"Walking Max!" I said louder.

"Really?" he said. "I wouldn't say no to that."

"Great!" I said.

"Maxie!" he called out. Then he kind of shuffled back inside.

And I thought—*cha-ching!* I'd been in business for two minutes and I already had my first customer.

"It's five dollars a walk!" I yelled inside. "And I'll need your leash! Also, I have my own bags. Those are included, no charge!"

"Just one sec," Mr. Schneider called back.

A whole bunch of seconds later, he came to the

door again. This time he had Max on a leash, and an empty plastic bag.

"You're going to want this," he said, and gave me the bag. "Maxie makes some big number twos."

"Uh...okay," I said, and shoved it in my pocket, even though I didn't need it. "Do you want me to walk him every day, or—"

"Well, that would be better than sliced steak!" he said. "I sure do appreciate this, Rafe."

"It's no problem," I told him.

"I wish I could pay you, but..."

"Wait—huh?" I said.

"Social Security just isn't what it used to be," he said. "You know how it is."

Actually, I didn't know anything just then. Including what had just happened. Because now I was holding Max's leash and Mr. Schneider was already closing the door.

It's not like I minded doing Mr. Schneider the favor. He was really nice, and it didn't seem like anyone ever came to visit him. It was just that... well, *duh*. You can't buy too many private jets with *favors*.

Then, before I could make a move, the door opened again.

"Hang on there, Rafe," he said. "I forgot to pull that quarter out of your ear."

"The what out of my what?" I asked.

"Nothing in my hand, see?" he said, and held it up to show me. Then he reached over by my head, and I heard this tiny *flick* sound before he pulled a quarter out of nowhere.

"How'd you do that?" I said.

"Same way you get to Carnegie Hall," he said.

"Huh?"

"Practice, practice, practice!" he said. Then he put the quarter in my hand. "That's for you, my friend."

I still didn't know what to do. I mean, what would *you* do? I figured I was stuck for at least one walk. I'd worry about the rest later. So I just said thanks and shoved that quarter in my pocket.

"I'll be back soon," I told him.

"Take your time," he said.

And I thought—*Yeah, right*. I didn't have time to take my time. I had to get back to making real money, ASAP.

CHAPTER 8

THE SWEET SMELL OF SUCCESS

By the end of winter break, I had three paying customers, on top of Mr. Schneider. (I didn't have the heart to tell him I was going to stop walking Max, so I just kept doing it.)

Mr. Tohtz said he could use some early-morning help with Chester. Mr. and Mrs. Johnston said they wanted me to come in the afternoons to take Marshmallow out for a squirt. And Mrs. Calhoun asked me to check with her once a week about helping take care of her two pugs, Frick and Frack.

I finally told Mom about all of it, and she thought it was great. She even said I could hand out some flyers at the Park and Bark.

So I did. And I came up with a real name for my business too.

DOGS TO GO
$5/walk
Rafe Khatchadorian
President

That didn't leave me much time to hang out at Flip's house, but I did spend the last Friday night of vacation over there. We played TrollQuest until midnight, when his parents told us to turn it off. Which we did, for about twenty minutes. Then we put on headphones and played until four in the morning. It was like a perfect night, except it made me want my own system even more.

Meanwhile, the money was adding up. By that Sunday, I had fifty-five bucks stuck in the shoe box in the back of my bottom desk drawer. And even though I was supposed to be saving, I told Mom I wanted to take everyone out to dinner.

We went to one of my favorite places, Dave & Buster's, and I paid for the whole thing.

"I'm impressed, Rafe," Mom said, and raised a glass of root beer so we could toast.

"Cheers, cheers, and cheers!" Grandma said, and clinked with everyone.

As for Georgia, I think she actually felt jealous of me for the first time in her life. So let's just say it was a pretty good night.

But of course, it couldn't last forever. Vacation was ending. School was starting up again.

And the Great Dog War was just around the corner.

period English, guess who was sitting at one of the desks, wearing a smug-looking smile?

"What are you doing here?" I said. "This is my class."

"Try '*our* class,'" Georgia said. "I'm going to be in here from now on. It's like permanent extra credit."

"You've got to be kidding me," I said.

"Not even a little," she said.

I couldn't believe it. Up to now, the one good thing about school was that my sister had her own grade and her own classes. In other words, it was the one place on earth where she was required *by law* to stay away from me.

Not anymore. Now I was going to be starting every day for the rest of the year with Georgia getting her brains all over me. It made me want to jump out the nearest window and start running.

"All right, people," Mrs. Stonecase said. "Let's get started. Rafe, where's your copy of *Island of the Blue Dolphins*?"

"It's in my locker," I said. "I'll go get it."

I figured I could eat up at least ten minutes of the period that way. But even that backfired.

"You can just look on with your sister," Mrs. Stonecase said. "Have a seat."

In other words, I was as deep into the Georgia zone as I could get now. *Great*.

"I'll bet this is driving you *crazy*," Georgia said.

"Whatever," I told her. I wasn't going to give her the satisfaction.

"Oh, and by the way—" she said.

"Quiet, please!" Mrs. Stonecase said. "Now, as we discuss this story, I want you all to think about three things…"

I didn't hear much after that except the sound of my sister's head getting bigger and bigger. Also, she kept nudging me and trying to get my attention. But I just kept my eyes down and locked on that book like she wasn't even there.

A minute later, I heard a scribbling sound next to me. Then this little note slid under my nose— *FWIP!*—right where I couldn't possibly miss it.

Which of course was the whole point.

CHAPTER 10

NEVER LET THEM SEE YOU SWEAT

By the time I got to lunch, I was feeling lower than Death Valley.

I managed to survive English and social studies with Georgia, but we still had sixth-period science to go. Not to mention the WHOLE REST OF THE SCHOOL YEAR.

On the bright side, I managed to come up with that new Loozer comic. I did it during silent reading in English when I was supposed to be figuring out what that *Island of the Blue Dolphins* was all about.

Believe it or not, people actually liked my Loozer stuff. Sure, some of the comics were kind of about me and my problems, which I don't always want everyone to know about. And my Leo the Silent character was based on my real-life twin brother, who died when we were three. Who knows what he would've been like, but in my mind he was a pretty great friend. That's something else I don't go blabbing about either. The other kids think I'm weird enough already.

Anyway, I'd been putting it in the school newspaper like a regular comic strip. The paper was called *Fine Print,* and I worked on it two days a week at lunch with Jeanne Galletta.

If you know my story, you know that:

1. I've been crazy about Jeanne from the day I met her.
2. She was more likely to fall in love with a whole-wheat bagel than she was with me.

3. After a couple of world-class disasters in the romance department, we became friends. And I mean like real friends, where I don't turn red and swallow my tongue when I try to talk to her. For me, that's a huge improvement.

So at lunch, I showed her the Brainzilla comic to see if it passed the Jeanne test. If she doesn't laugh, I don't put it in the paper.

"This is funny," Jeanne said.

"Cool, I'll scan it in," I said.

"*Well…*" she said. "This is about Georgia, right?" she said. "I heard she got put into some of your classes, and—"

"You *heard* that?" I asked. "From who?"

But I was pretty sure I already knew the answer. *Georgia!* Seriously, my sister's mouth could have its own twenty-four-hour news channel.

"It's none of my business, Rafe, but do you really want the whole school knowing how you feel about this?" Jeanne asked.

"Is it that obvious?" I said.

"Kind of," she said. Which was just a nice way of saying *yes*.

So I crumpled up that comic and threw it in the trash. Right before I took it back out and stuck it in my backpack. I'm not saying Georgia could *actually* sniff it out like a bloodhound on steroids. But on the other hand, why take chances?

Oh well. Back to the drawing board.

CHAPTER 11

FAKE IT TILL YOU MAKE IT

I probably should have left the whole thing alone. But if you have a little brother or sister, you might know how it is. Sometimes they're just *begging* to be messed with. Am I right?

I couldn't out-brainiac Georgia, but I could still get inside her head. So by the time we sat down for dinner that night, I knew just what I wanted to do.

It started when Mom was dishing up the jalapeño meatloaf (yum!) and Georgia started yakking about how she'd gotten bumped into my classes.

"Well, that's wonderful," Grandma said. "Maybe you two can work on your homework together."

"Speaking of homework," I said, "after dinner, I'm going to need a hammer, a roll of masking tape, and an orange for science."

"What science? We don't have any science homework," Georgia said right away—just like a fish chomping down on a fat, juicy worm.

Now all I had to do was reel her in.

"It's for the science fair," I said.

"What science fair?" Georgia kept going.

But I didn't say anything after that. I just went back to mowing down my meatloaf.

Because here's what else I knew about my sister. It didn't matter if she mostly believed me or not. All I needed was one tiny little doubt. That was enough to drive her crazy.

I mean, even crazier than she already was.

So when I was done eating, I just collected up my fake science stuff and headed to my room. Sure enough, once I closed the door, it was like five, four, three, two—

KNOCK KNOCK KNOCK!

"Rafe?" Georgia yelled.

I pulled off a long piece of masking tape and wrapped one end around the orange. Then I started swinging it around like I was testing it for gravity or something.

"You can come in," I said, and she did.

"There's not *really* a science fair," she said. "Right?"

"What does it look like?" I said.

"I think you're just making this up to annoy me," she said.

"Hmmm," I said, and started swinging that orange in the opposite direction. "That *does* sound like something I'd do. But I guess we'll find out tomorrow."

"*Please?* Just tell me yes or no," she said. You could practically smell the desperation in the air.

"Rafe!" Mom yelled from the living room. "Does she have science homework or not?"

Oh well. It was fun while it lasted.

"Nah," I told Georgia. "I was just messing with you, but that's because you kept opening your big mouth about—"

"*MOM!*" Georgia screamed. "Did you hear that? Rafe totally made it up!"

"Work it out, you two," Mom said. "I'm not going to referee anymore."

"I'll referee!" Grandma Dotty said, but Mom just turned up the TV.

Now Georgia was standing there, squinting at

me like she had acid shooting out of her eyes.

"What?" I said.

"You heard her," she said. "We need to work this out."

"I think we just did," I said.

"Well, *I* think—" Georgia said. Right before I closed the door. I'm pretty sure she got the message, anyway.

Don't Mess with the Rafe.

CHAPTER 12

CHA-CHING!

Meanwhile, my dog-walking business had gone from good to *wow*. Maybe it was all that TrollQuest I'd been playing, but the whole thing felt like the world's best video game. The more dogs I walked, the more points I earned.

And in this case, the points were cold, hard CA$H. That's my kind of game!

I had six regular customers now, a hundred and four bucks in the bank, and another ninety-eight stashed in my drawer at home. I could just taste that brand-new WormHole Premium system already. Everything was full steam ahead...

Right up until the next day, when I got to the dog park and stepped in a steaming pile of trouble.

See, they have this community bulletin board

at the Park and Bark. It's a place where you can post ads about missing cats, or alien sightings, or anything you want. That's where I had a copy of my Dogs To Go poster.

Except when I got there, some jerk had taken mine down and put a brand-new poster in its place. And this one had bad news written all over it.

As soon as I saw that, my brain started to boil. Competition was one thing, but ripping down my stuff was like starting a fight.

So I fought back.

I reached out and tore that Cheap Walks flyer right off the board.

"HEY!" someone yelled. "Is that yours?"

I looked over and it was Nose Ring Guy.

"I was just moving it," I said.

"Didn't look that way to me," he said.

I didn't say anything, mostly because Nose Ring Guy has arms about the size of my head. I just smoothed out that Cheap Walks flyer and put it back up.

But I wasn't done being mad. Not even close.

So I let Junior and Marshmallow run around until Nose Ring Guy was gone. Then I went back over to the bulletin board.

I looked left. I looked right. I made sure nobody else was there to yell at me.

Then I took down that poster again, and this time, I threw it in the trash.

Later, Cheap Walks!

Just for the record, I'm not saying that was

a good move, or a smart thing to do. I know two wrongs don't make a right, and all that. But sometimes when I get mad, I don't exactly think straight. And when I don't think straight, I do dumb things.

Like messing with someone else's property when I shouldn't.

Or thinking that nobody's watching me when they actually are.

Or stepping right into the middle of a war.

You know—stuff like that.

CHAPTER 13

MAGIC MURRAY

Come in, come in, my friend!" Mr. Schneider said when I came to pick up Max that day. "I have something I want to show you."

Mr. Schneider's apartment always looked like a junkyard to me. If he'd had a mom living there, she would have made him clean it up a long time ago.

But here's the thing about junkyards. Once you look a little closer, they can be pretty cool places.

His living room was like a workshop. He had a big table with a bunch of tools and loose parts spread out, and those bendy lights that can go any way you want them.

He also had stuff all over his walls. There were pictures in frames, an old calendar, and a whole bunch of posters from different magic shows. I even recognized one name, Harry Houdini. But the biggest poster showed some guy called Magic Murray.

"Did you ever see that guy?" I asked.

"Only every time I look in the mirror," Mr. Schneider said.

"No way," I said. "That's *you?*"

"Well, yes and no," he said. "I *was* Magic Murray. Now I'm just Murray Schneider, retired magician and full-time old fogey."

That explained the quarter trick, anyway. Also why Mr. Schneider looked about eight and a half times older than the guy on the poster.

"Hang on one sec," he said, and started going through some drawers. He took out a scarf, a bunch of metal cups, some fake flowers, three gloves, and finally, a pair of handcuffs.

"Take a close look," he said, and gave me the cuffs. "No cracks, no tricks, no funny business. Am I right?"

Next, he held out his hands and told me to put the cuffs on him.

"Seriously?" I said.

"Serious as a drought in a fishbowl," he told me. So I did.

"Now I want you to point at those cuffs and wave your hand over them three times. Not four times, not twice, but three times exactly. We can't afford any explosions in here."

I knew he was kidding around, but I played along. I reached out and waved my hand back and forth, once—

"Dallas," he said.

—twice—

"Springfield," he said.

—three times.

"Kalamazoo!"

And I swear, those cuffs flew right off. He didn't move or anything. One second they were on his wrists, and the next, they were on the floor.

"Not bad, right?" he said. He even took a little bow.

"Will you show me how you did that?" I asked.

"I just showed you," he said. "It's magic, not rocket science."

"Come on, please?" I said.

I knew it wasn't *actually* magic, but I wanted to know how those cuffs worked. And then I wanted to start using them to mess with Georgia's mind.

"Sorry, Rafe," Mr. Schneider said. "A magician never tells his secrets. But you can keep the quarter."

"What quarter?" I said.

"The one under your foot," he said.

Sure enough, I took a step back and there it was, right where I'd been standing the whole time. Wow!

I mean, it still wasn't as nice as a five-dollar bill, but I was starting to think there might be another way Magic Murray could pay me for all that dog-walking.

CHAPTER 14

THE TRUCE IS LOOSE

I was pulling a snack out of the fridge later and I got blindsided, big-time. You know that thing in scary movies where someone closes a door and the psycho killer is standing right there?

That was Georgia. For a loudmouth, she sure can move quietly.

Annoyed to Death IV
The Last Nerve

By the time you see her coming, you're already DEAD.

"What do you want?" I said.

"Listen, Rafe," Georgia told me. "I know you don't want me in your classes, and all that. But I was thinking about what Mom said—"

"You mean when she told you I was her favorite?"

"Very funny," she said. "Here's my idea. You help me take out the garbage tonight, and I'll help you get ready for tomorrow's English quiz. You know, like a truce. And we make sure Mom sees us doing all of it together."

I liked the idea of making Mom happy. And I knew Georgia hated doing the garbage. But I also didn't trust my sister any farther than I could throw an overweight elephant up a steep hill.

"What makes you think I need your help?" I said.

"Did you even finish the book?" she said.

"Maybe."

"Yeah, I didn't think so," she said.

The problem was, I *hadn't* finished. I was thinking maybe I'd stay up all night getting it done, but...who am I kidding? That wasn't ever going to happen.

Also, Mrs. Stonecase is famous for her killer essay quizzes. It's like she's allergic to multiple choice or something.

"Yeah, okay," I said. "For Mom's sake. But you help me first and *then* I help you."

"Deal," Georgia said.

So we waited for Mom to come home. Then Georgia told me all about what happens at the end of *Island of the Blue Dolphins*. After that, we took out the trash.

"This is good to see," Mom said. "Nice cooperation, you two."

Georgia gave me one of her told-you-so looks, but I didn't care. I just wanted Mom to be happy.

Also, we'd spent at least half an hour studying for that quiz and less than ten minutes taking out the trash. In other words, I totally came out ahead on this one. Score another point for the Rafe.

Boo-yah!

CHAPTER 15

ENGLISH QUIZ DEATH MATCH

Have a seat, take out a pen, and leave the rest of your things on the floor," Mrs. Stonecase said when we came into English the next morning.

Nobody takes quizzes more seriously than she does. But here's the cool part. Now that I had a piece of Georgia's brain on my side, I felt like I was wearing an F-proof suit for this one.

Sure enough, as soon as I got a look at those essay questions, I actually knew what I wanted to say for all three of them, right away. The last time that happened…

Actually, that *never* happens. Not for me, anyway.

But this time, I was ready to rumble!

AND IN THIS CORNER, WEIGHING IN AT THREE PAGES OF DEATH-DEFYING ESSAY QUESTIONS, WE HAVE CHARLOTTE P. STONECASE'S LEAN... MEAN QUIZZING MACHINE!
Hit him where it hurts.
I got this.
QUIZ
AT THE SOUND OF THE BELL, COME OUT SWINGING WITH GLOVES UP. AND MAY THE BEST KID - OR QUIZ - WIN!
DINGGG!!
ROUND 1
In Island of the Blue Dolphins, does Karana make the right choice to stay on the island with her brother? Why or why not?

I come out of my corner fast. I go at this thing like it's made out of steak and I'm a starving man. Right swing! Left hook! Jab-jab-jab! I get it up against the ropes and keep on swinging so it knows I mean business. The way it's going so far, I'm going to make this quiz wish it had never been born.

Next question!

I don't slow down, even for a second. I keep coming with everything I've got, light on my feet and heavy with my hands. I dodge! I slide! I dance! I weave! I'm pulling out moves even *I* didn't know I had, while I answer this thing to within an inch of its life.

Next question!

Happy ending? Yeah, you bet. For *me*. We're in the home stretch now, and I've got this thing right where I want it. As soon as I spot my opening, I make my final move. *WHAM!* The whole thing comes down like a little pig's straw house. And as far as I can tell, it's not getting up again.

In fact, the whole thing's over so quick, this crowd is going to be screaming for their money back. But ask me if I care.

Because I just scored myself the world's easiest knockout.

CHAPTER 16

NOT EVEN CLOSE

So let's just say I finished that quiz feeling pretty good. There were a couple of things I didn't remember from what Georgia had told me, but I was still thinking I had a solid B+ coming. Maybe even an A.

"Does anyone have any questions about the quiz?" Mrs. Stonecase asked after everyone handed theirs in.

Usually, I keep my mouth shut for that kind of thing. But this time, I went for it. Even Mrs. S looked surprised when my hand went up.

"Yes, Rafe?" she said.

"On number three, does it matter if I couldn't remember the name of the oil company?" I asked.

"Excuse me?" Mrs. Stonecase said.

"The one at the end of the story. You know—the oil company that takes over the island and gives Karana a job," I told her.

"A *job?*" she said.

"Yeah, at the Blue Dolphin Café?" I asked. "I remembered everything else, so I'm hoping it doesn't take too many points off if I..."

But then I stopped, because Mrs. Stonecase was looking at me like one of us had forgotten how to speak English.

"I assume this is some kind of joke, Rafe," she said.

Maybe that's why some of the other kids were laughing, I wasn't sure. But something was definitely wrong. I looked over at Georgia, and she was too busy scribbling on a piece of paper to notice.

"Did you even read the book?" Mrs. S asked me.

"Um...yes?" I said.

"Well, I hope you read the next one more carefully," she said. Then she started handing out our copies of *A Long Walk to Water*.

A second later, Madison Walker tapped me on the shoulder and passed me a note. It had my name on it in Georgia's handwriting. And when I unfolded it, there was just one single word inside.

Which is when I realized how badly I'd blown it. And I don't just mean on the quiz. Because I'd also broken the number one rule when it comes to dealing with Georgia.

Rule #1: NEVER TRUST GEORGIA.

CHAPTER 17

CHOICES, CHOICES

If that was Georgia's way of paying me back for my little science fair fake-out, then I obviously wasn't being creative enough.

Lucky for me, creative is my specialty.

I spent the rest of the day thinking about my next move—and thinking bigger.

Like for instance, maybe I'd give her whole room the Saran wrap treatment—with bonus points for doing it while she was asleep.

Or maybe I'd go old-school. There's definitely something to say for the classics. Like for instance, I'm a big fan of the twenty-one-pizza salute.

Then again, maybe it made more sense to come up with something all new. Something nobody had ever seen before. The possibilities were endless, really. It's like Mom says sometimes—the only limitation is my imagination.

Whatever it was going to be, I wanted to take my time and be careful choosing it. Until then, I knew Georgia would always be wondering when it would happen. That was a little bit of torture in itself.

The problem was, all of that was about to fly out the window. The next big move was going to choose *me*. And when it did, it was going to make my little battle with Georgia seem like the world's smallest potatoes.

In other words, the Great Dog War had already started.

I just didn't know it yet.

CHAPTER 18

BiG TROUBLE iN DOGTOWN

When I got out of school that day, it was ten degrees and snowing like crazy. It looked like the whole world had a bad case of dandruff.

But when I got to the Johnstons' house to pick up Marshmallow, Mrs. Johnston looked totally confused to see me.

"Rafe?" she said. "What are you doing out in this weather? You sounded terrible on the phone."

"I did?" I said.

"Yes, not at all like yourself. I thought you were sick," she said.

"I'm okay," I said. But something weird was going on, because I'd never called Mrs. Johnston.

"Well, I'm sorry you came all this way," she said. "But your sub was just here. He already walked Marshmallow and we're all set for today."

It was getting weirder by the second. First, she was talking about phone calls I never made. And now I supposedly had a substitute?

The thing was, I didn't want Mrs. Johnston to know how clueless I was. Not until I figured this out. So I tried to play it cool, which wasn't that hard in ten-degree weather.

"Did you see which way he went?" I asked.

"Sorry, no," she said. "But he did say today's walk was free and that the price would be four dollars from now on."

And—BAM! Another piece of the puzzle landed like a boulder on my brain. That Cheap Walks flyer had said something about the first walk being free and then four dollars after that.

This was getting very real, very fast. Whoever this kid was, he'd started coming after *my* business. And he'd even impersonated me on the phone to do it.

"Rafe?" Mrs. Johnston waved a hand in front of my face. "You don't seem well, honey. Why don't you go home and get back in bed?"

"Yeah, okay. Good idea," I said. I even threw in

a little cough to make it convincing.

But then I booked it straight over to the Calhouns' house instead. And sure enough—

"Rafe? What are you doing here?" Mr. Calhoun said. "Your sub just picked up Frick and Frack a minute ago."

That was it. I'd officially been *sub-otaged*.

"Did you see which way he went?" I asked.

"Sure," Mr. Calhoun said, and pointed up the street. "I think that's him right there."

When I looked, I saw some jerk at the top of the block, walking Frick and Frack around the corner and out of sight.

"Okaythanksalot!" I said.

Then I took off after him like my business empire, my bank account, and my WormHole Premium Multi-Platform GameBox depended on it.

Which they basically did.

CHAPTER 19

DOUBLE TROUBLE

I wasn't just regular mad anymore. Now I was *fighting* mad. If you've ever taken a punch, you'll know what I'm talking about.

I booked up the street as fast as I could. The snow was up to my knees, so I wasn't exactly clocking Olympic time, but I kept moving.

I went around the corner.

Up the next block.

Onto another street.

And that's where I finally spotted him. Kind of. Because this is where things got weird.

Now the kid was coming back down the street, like he'd just turned around from wherever he'd been. Which wasn't the weird part. The thing was, he had three completely different dogs with him.

It was like he'd slipped around the corner, traded in Frick and Frack, and come back the other way, all in about a minute and a half.

What...the...dog???

I'd never seen this kid before, but it didn't even matter. I was so confused by now, I didn't feel ready for anything.

Before he could spot me, I jumped behind one of the snowplow piles on the side of the road. Then I made like a snow mole and got myself as far out of sight as I could.

"Hey!" the kid yelled.

I thought he'd spotted me, so I almost stood back up. But first, I took a quick peek. And that's when I saw who he was actually yelling for.

You know that expression, "I couldn't believe my eyes"? That was me just then. Because what I saw was an exact copy of the same kid, walking up the street with Frick and Frack. (Have you figured it out yet?)

Yeah, that's right. Cheap Walks was identical twins! The whole thing was like a magic trick, without the quarter or the handcuffs.

All of a sudden it was two against one, and I

didn't feel so much like fighting anymore. So I stuck myself into that snowbank as deep I could. Then I stayed low and waited for them to walk their thieving butts around the next corner.

This was definitely war now. But I needed to be readier for it than I was. And that meant it was time to call in the reinforcements. I didn't have a twin brother of my own anymore, at least not outside my comics, but I did have someone who'd always had my back.

Also known as Flip.

CHAPTER 20

DOING IT RIGHT

So there I am, half an hour later in Flip's basement, racing to the top of the Bottomless Caverns of D'Enth. I'm picking up all the gold nuggets I can find, but I'm watching out, too. In TrollQuest, you never know when the next gnarly, slimy, or super-weaponized enemy is going to come running around the corner to destroy you.

Which, when you think about it, wasn't so different from my dog-walking problem.

And you're probably thinking, *Yo, Rafe, didn't you have a huge emergency you wanted to talk to Flip about, like, three paragraphs ago?*

Well, yeah. But just because I had a war on my hands doesn't mean I had to skip the best part about being at Flip's house.

"So what's the plan?" Flip asked me.

"I want to find as much gold as I can," I said, "Once we level up, I think we can trade it in for—"

"No, I mean with those Cheap Walks losers," Flip said. "If you ask me, you ought to pound them like a pair of railroad spikes."

"I don't know about that," I said. Now that I'd had a chance to cool off, I didn't want to pound anyone (or be pounded by them, either). Not anymore. I just wanted to protect my business.

And to be honest, I wasn't completely listening to Flip. We'd just run around a bend in the cave and right into a pod of skeleton zombies. Those are the worst kind. You shatter one of them with your sword, and all you get is a hundred reanimated skeleton parts coming after you from a hundred different directions. Believe me, you only make that mistake once.

"Get out of there!" Flip yelled.

"I am!" I said, and we both headed back to the main cavern to look for another way up.

"Okay, so what next?" I said.

"Maybe you should fight fire with fire," Flip said. "Find out who Cheap Walks' customers are and pick them off—"

"I mean in the game!" I said.

"Oh," Flip said. "In that case, hang on."

He spun his axe around five or six times and smashed a hole right into the cavern ceiling. We ran up the pile of rubble it made, knocked down the pile behind us, and kept going.

"What do you think would happen if I just tried talking to those guys?" I said.

"You can't talk to skeleton zombies," Flip said. "They don't even have ears."

"No, the Cheap Walks guys," I said.

"Huh?" Flip said.

Finally, I paused the game. Maybe we needed to focus on one thing at a time.

"I was just wondering if I should go over there and talk it out, face-to-face," I said. "You know, like adults."

"Seriously?" Flip said.

"Seriously," I said. I'd been thinking about Mom too. And I knew that was what she'd want me to do.

Flip just shrugged like that was some kind of crazy new idea. Then he took the game off Pause and we started running again.

"Whatever you want, it's your call," he said. "Just tell me where to go, what to do, and who *not* to pound."

And that's what makes Flip such a great best friend. Because he always has my back—in the game *and* in the real world.

CHAPTER 21

THE FACE-OFF

As soon as we got out of school the next day, Flip came home with me to pick up Junior. Then we went over to get Marshmallow and go out for a walk like usual.

But we didn't go in the usual direction. Now that I knew how to sniff out those Cheap Walks rats, I went right for their neighborhood.

It didn't take long to get a nose full of rat either. We were coming up the same block as the last time, and there he was. One of them, anyway. He was walking two little brown dogs down someone's driveway.

"HEY—CHEAP WALKS!" Flip yelled.

The kid stopped and turned around. When

he saw us, he pulled a coach's whistle out of his pocket and blew it, really loud.

It must have been a signal, because two seconds later the other twin came flying around the corner with a big black Lab on a leash.

And I thought—*Man, these twerps really know what they're doing.*

About five seconds later, the four of us were standing there on the sidewalk, face-to-face-to-face-to-face. You could have cut the tension with a plastic knife.

And yeah, I'll admit it. I might have been thinking a little bit about TrollQuest again. They even looked a little like trolls

"What do you want?" the twin on the right said.

"I'm Dogs To Go," I said. "And I came over to say it's not cool to steal another guy's customers."

The two of them looked at each other like I'd told some kind of joke or something.

"Ohhh, we're sowwy," Righty said.

"What?" I said.

"Did we hurt your widdle feewings?" Lefty said. And then they both cracked up.

"Are you kidding me with this?" Flip said.
"It's called doing business in America. Get used to it," Lefty said. "And besides, you tore down our poster at the dog park about two minutes after we put it up."

"Only because you tore *mine* down, dude!" I said.

"I'm not your dude, *dude!*" Lefty said. "And we didn't even see your dumb poster. It probably ripped itself down because it was ashamed of its own lameness."

"Sure you didn't," Flip said. "And yours just *happened* to go up in the exact same spot. Don't even try."

"Are you calling him a liar?" Righty said.

"More like half a liar," Flip said, then pointed at Righty. "And you're the other half."

"Shut up," Lefty told him.

"No, *you* shut up," I said.

"Okay, that's it," Flip said. And he went for them both.

I started to pull Flip back, but that sidewalk was like an ice rink. My foot hit an extra-slick patch, and I went down hard. Plus, Junior's leash got tangled in the black Lab's leash just before Lefty came at me, and missed, and hit the dirt too. Or the ice, I guess.

I managed to get out of his way, but I tripped up Righty when I did, and pretty soon we were all just one big knot of arms, legs, dogs, and leashes.

"Get off me!" one of the twins said.

"I'm not on you," I said.

"Woof!"

"Ruff!"

"Just MOVE, you doofus!"

"If I could move, I would."

"Get your stinkin' elbow out of my ear."

"Get your stinkin' *breath* out of my *face*."

"What?"

"WOOF!"

It wasn't *exactly* like that. Some of the words were the kind that can earn you a detention in school. But you get the idea.

By the time we untangled ourselves, I was out of breath, super ticked off, and, to be honest, a little bit relieved. No one had thrown any punches, but I wasn't sure how long that was going to last. And I had just enough brains to know that going all MMA fighter on each other wasn't going to cut it either.

So we just took our dogs and got out of there. Talking to those guys obviously wasn't going to work. It was time to put Plan A in the trash and start dusting off Plan B instead.

Or maybe I should call it Plan M. For Mom.

CHAPTER 22

PLAN M

Hey, Mom, what do you do when you have a problem with someone?" I asked her that night.

Mom stopped stirring the chili she was making and looked at me like the fire alarm had just gone off.

"Did you get in a fight?" she asked.

"No," I said.

"You can tell me—"

"I didn't get in a fight," I said. Technically, it was true.

"Okay, good," she said. She looked relieved and started chopping onions.

"I'm not asking about a *fight-fight*. I mean more like a conflict," I said. "Like if someone was stealing your shifts at the diner, what would you do?"

"Well, first of all, people can't 'steal' my shifts," she said. "But if someone tried, I wouldn't let them get away with it."

"Yeah, but *how?*" I said. I could imagine some possibilities, but not any realistic ones.

"Well, I'd either talk to Swifty, or to the other person directly," Mom told me. Then she gave me this look that said—*Okay, mister. I answered your question. Now it's time to answer mine.*

"Why are we talking about this, Rafe?" she asked.

I knew that was coming. So I told her the whole thing, about Cheap Walks, and how I *did* try to talk to them, and how that had gone about as well as a campfire in a helium balloon.

When I was done, Mom looked at me like I'd just told her I'd climbed Mount Everest. Without oxygen. Or feet.

"You really *are* getting more mature, aren't you?" she said. Then she gave me a big hug, and a kiss too. Which was more credit than I deserved.

"Thanks," I said.

"Unfortunately, I don't think you're going to like what comes next," Mom said. "But it's time for me to call these boys' parents."

"*WHAT?*" I said. "What happened to not playing referee?"

"Let's just say I take that on a case-by-case basis," Mom told me. "Stealing your customers is *not* okay."

Yeah, I thought, but neither was getting my mommy to fight my battles for me.

Now it was too late. Before you could say "NO NO NO, PLEASE DON'T DO THIS, YOU'RE GIVING THEM EVEN MORE AMMUNITION AGAINST ME!," Mom was on the phone calling Cheap Walks.

It was my own fault, I guess. I was the one who thought it was a good idea to talk to Mom in the first place. At least, part of me thought so. The other part was ready to strangle the first part. Because *that* guy never knows when to keep his stupid mouth shut.

CHAPTER 23

SUMMIT MEETING

So Mom set up a meeting at Cheap Walks' house and we had to go over there the next night, when I was supposed to be playing TQ with Flip. That's like trading in a trip to Disney World for a dentist's appointment. With twin dentists.

Not that I had much choice.

It turned out they lived only a couple of blocks from our house. And when their mom answered the door, she was totally friendly too.

"Hello, I'm Cora Finn," the lady said. "You'll have to excuse the mess. I just got home from work, and there's never enough time for cleaning."

"Believe me, I know how that is," Mom said, and just like that, the two of them were all insta-buddy-buddy.

I followed them into the living room, and that's where I came face-to-face with the matching scumbags again.

"Rafe, this is Eddie and Ethan," Mrs. Finn said. "Say hello, boys."

"Hi," I said.

"Hi," they said. I kind of expected some evil eye, but they just acted normal. Probably because of the mom factor. I didn't forget they were total fakes, though. They weren't fooling me.

"Boys, take the Khatchadorians' coats, please," Mrs. Finn told them. "And would everyone like some hot cider?"

It was almost like we were there for a party or something. But unless we were going to play Pin-the-Blame-on-the-Twins, I wasn't interested.

After that, the two moms did most of the talking. That's when I found out that Ethan and Eddie went to West Middle School, but they'd just moved into our neighborhood from across town.

"Next week, they'll be transferring to HVMS!" Mrs. Finn said, like that was supposed to be a good thing. It just kept getting worse. The last thing I needed at school was two more problems.

So I fired up my cyborg brain, hacked into the school computer's mainframe, canceled their registration, and gave both of them an extensive criminal record while I was at it.

You know…or not.

More like *I wish*.

Anyway, all you really need to know is that by the time our "meeting" was over, we had some new rules.

1. No stealing anyone's customers.

2. No touching anyone else's signs. We still didn't agree about who started it, but Mom and Mrs. Finn said that didn't even matter anymore. (Even though it did, if you ask me.)

And number three was the big one.

"This is going to be the first and last time we do this," Mrs. Finn said.

"If we have to step in again, trust me, nobody's going to like it," Mom said.

"That's okay with me," I said. Mostly I just wanted to get back to making money without the twins of doom cutting into my profits.

"Yeah, okay," Eddie said.

"That's fair," Ethan said.

I was finally starting to figure them out too. Ethan had a bigger nose and Eddie always talked first.

"Now shake on it," Mrs. Finn said.

So I went ahead and shook hands with both of them. Because I'm an idiot. And I don't mean for making a deal with those two. I mean, I'm an idiot because I actually believed they were making a deal with me.

Well, guess what?

They weren't.

CHAPTER 24

LET'S (NOT) MAKE A DEAL

Guess how long it took for Cheap Walks to strike again.

Three days?

Two days?

Fourteen and a half hours?

Wrong! They'd *already* struck before me and Mom even left their house, if you can believe that.

So there I was the next day, walking Junior and Marshmallow, just minding my own business.

And speaking of "business," about halfway to the dog park, Junior stopped and did some of his own. I pulled a baggie out of my coat pocket, stuck my hand inside, bent down to pick it up like usual, and—

EWWWWWWWWWWWW!

Yeah. There was a big hole in the bag. Exactly what you're thinking might have happened... happened.

I used about a ton and a half of snow to clean off my hand. By the time I finished, my fingers were blue. And numb. If I could have boiled that hand, I would have.

Meanwhile, I still had Junior's business to pick up, so I pulled out another bag, and—*riii-iiiip!* My hand went right through that one too.

I always kept a supply in my coat, but when I checked, I saw that every single bag had been cut along the bottom.

That's when I started putting two and two together. And it added up to...

Cheap Walks.

It wasn't like I needed an official note from Eddie and Ethan to figure out they were behind this. But guess what? There was one of those too. Right at the bottom of my pocket.

So much for making a deal.

CHAPTER 25

WHAT NEXT?

As soon as I got to the dog park, I let Junior and Marshmallow off their leashes and sat down to think.

I'm not going to lie. I was starting to wonder if maybe the problem was *me*. I've never been the world's leading expert at "getting along well with others," if you know what I mean. Maybe it was time to take a good long look in the mirror.

And I would. Definitely. Real soon.

But in the meantime, I was mostly thinking about what Ethan and Eddie would look like hanging in a giant, sticky web, waiting to be turned into a two-course meal for an army of yellow-eyed spider freaks.

And I can just hear them now.

"HELP MEEEEEEE!"

"I'M SCAAAAAARED!!"

"I CAN'T MOOOOOVE!"

"I JUST WET MY PAAAAAAANTS!"

Which is exactly when I happen to stumble across them, right there in the middle of my own daydream-quest.

"Well, well, well. Look who wandered into my world," I say. "Seems like you two could use a little Troll 911."

"You have to help us!" Eddie says.

"Get us down from here!" Ethan begs.

Meanwhile, I'm holding on to my axe, which of course is more than strong enough to cut them loose.

I mean, if I feel like it.

"You know, you really shouldn't shout like that," I say. "Those spider folks have great hearing." Then I check over my shoulder, where I can just see the first few pairs of yellow eyes starting to emerge from the woods. "I think you're running out of time too."

"Please!" Eddie says.

"We'll do *anything!*" Ethan says.

And I nod, and let them sweat just a little more, while the eight-legged army creeps in a little closer…a little closer…a little closer…

"Okay, tell you what," I say. "I'll cut you loose. But in exchange, I'm going to need you to leave the planet, never come back—oh, and wash my troll car before you go. Deal?"

"Deal!" Eddie says.

"Just hurry!" Ethan says, and I can see the relief in their beady little eyes as I raise my axe to cut them down.

But then I stop again.

"Actually," I say, "I'm still not a hundred percent sure I can trust you. So I think I'm going to need all that in writing. Either of you have a pen?"

"NO!" they both blubber at the same time.

"Oh…gosh," I say. "Well, that's too bad. For you, anyway. I guess that means—"

"HEY, KID! I'M TALKING TO YOU!" someone yelled.

When I looked up from my park bench, I had Big Beard, Puffy Coat, and Candy Crush all staring at me like I'd farted in church or something.

"Huh?" I said, coming back to earth.

"You left the gate open again!" Puffy Coat said.

"No, I didn't!" I said.

Except—maybe I did. My mind had been flying when I got to the park. Now I couldn't even remember what I'd done. Or hadn't done.

And speaking of not paying attention, that's when I figured out what the *real* problem was. Because Big Beard had just latched the gate. Marshmallow was sitting there looking at me like he needed someone to play with.

And as for Junior?

He was gone, gone, gone.

CHAPTER 26

MOVING TARGET

I went tearing out of that dog park as fast I could on six legs (if you count me and Marshmallow together).

"Excuse-me-did-you-see-a-brown-and-white-dog-go-by-here?" I asked the first lady I saw.

"Actually, yes," she said. "He went that way—"

We flew up the next block, looked both ways, kept going, and sprinted to the corner after that. Which is when I saw him.

"JUNIOR!" I yelled, but he kept on running.

The problem was, Junior loved this game. It's called Moving Target, and the whole idea is for him to run around like crazy while I try to catch him. Usually, we play it in the backyard or at the park where there's a fence to slow him down. Now, he basically had all of planet Earth to work with, and let's just say Junior was going for the *win*.

I'm pretty fast, thanks to all the training I've had from football and being chased by Miller the Killer, but Junior was even faster. Before I could get anywhere near him, he ducked around the corner of an apartment building and disappeared again.

I sped up and made Marshmallow go even faster. We hit the next corner, cut a hard right, and—*WHAM!*—plowed right into a policeman on the sidewalk. He was holding on to Junior's collar.

The good news was, no more Moving Target.

And the bad news? Well, the policeman was about six feet tall, wearing a badge, and giving me a look that said *You're not going to like this next part one bit.*

"This your dog?" the cop asked.

"Yeah!" I said. "Thanks!"

"Don't thank me," the cop said. "I'm writing you a ticket."

"What?" I said. "But I don't even drive."

"It's for having your dog off-leash in a public area," he said.

"How much is the ticket?" I asked.

"Forty-five dollars," he said. "You kids need to learn some responsibility around here."

It was like a punch to the gut. Or at least, to the bank account. I was actually going to *lose* money that afternoon. This was turning out to be one of the worst days I'd had in a long time.

And guess what? The day wasn't over.

Which meant there was still time for it to get worse.

CHAPTER 27

SOUP'S ON!

By now, I was on a street I'd never been on before. So I was hustling back toward my own neighborhood when I saw someone who looked a whole lot like Grandma Dotty, coming the other way.

In fact, it *was* Grandma. I just didn't know what she was doing in this part of town. But before I could figure it out, she opened a door and went inside some building.

Which was just as well. I didn't need Mom finding out that I'd chased Junior halfway across town. So I kept on walking.

When I got closer, I saw it was a church. There were some other people going in there too, including a guy with an old shopping cart that he left by the bike rack.

Now I was curious. So I tied Junior's and Marshmallow's leashes to a parking meter and went inside for a quick look.

The door Grandma used took me down some stairs to the basement, instead of up into the regular part of the church.

"Hello!" some lady said, and handed me a lunch tray.

"Is this a restaurant?" I asked her, and she smiled like I'd just said something nice.

"Enjoy your dinner," she said. Which was weird. I felt like I was on some kind of undercover mission, except I didn't know what the mission was.

When I got through the next door, a bunch of people were waiting in line with their trays. It looked kind of familiar, like the place our family volunteered at a few times when we lived in the city.

And I thought—*Oh, that's what it is*. Grandma was volunteering at a soup kitchen.

Except, she wasn't doing that either. Not unless they needed volunteers to stand in line with trays and get free food. Which is what she was actually doing.

And that was the weirdest part.

I mean, I know we aren't rich. *Duh*. That's why Mom had to work on Christmas. It's also why I get free lunch at school.

But this was different. I don't know why, it just was.

Seeing Grandma in that line felt like getting hit with a whole sampler platter of crazy feelings. I was kind of confused, and surprised, and sad, and even a little bit scared. All at the same time.

Mom didn't tell us about how bad things were because she never wanted us to worry. Maybe it was a lot worse than I thought.

Maybe we'd be homeless soon.

On top of all that, something told me this was supposed to be a secret. But from who? Did Mom even know?

And since I wasn't sure, the only thing that made sense was to get out of there, ASAP.

Also, AIAP—as incognito as possible. I really didn't want Grandma to see me.

So I used my tray for cover, turned around, and started swimming upstream in that line of people.

By the time I hit the sidewalk again, I was wiped out. What a day! I had Cheap Walks on the warpath, a forty-five-dollar ticket to pay, and now I'd just found out that my grandma was running around with a secret identity. And not in the cool way.

Put it like this. When getting a handful of dog poo *isn't* the worst part of your afternoon, you've got problems.

And I sure did. With a capital *P*.

CHAPTER 28

TRUST(UN)WORTHY

On my way home, I stopped at the Duper Market and got myself some M&M's and a can of Zoom. Then I got a bag of dog food, a bunch of bananas, a quart of milk, and a loaf of bread—the healthy kind Mom likes us to eat, with the whole grains and twigs and stuff.

Moo-licious

COW -A- Bunga

Chicky-kita bananas

kibbleZone DOG GRUB

Contains at least a tiny bit of real, actual meat! (Usually)

Back to the Earth, Extra-EXTRA Whole Grain Bread

With the wholesome taste of tree bark, grass and just a touch of dirt, because it's GOOD for you!

The trick was sneaking it all into the house so nobody would notice. Especially Mom.

And I was just about to pull it off too. There I was, pouring the quart of milk into a half-gallon container we already had in the fridge, when Georgia popped up out of nowhere, like the annoying little jack-in-the-box she is.

"Why are you doing that?" she said.

"STOP SNEAKING UP ON ME!" I yelled. I even spilled a bunch of milk on the floor.

"I'm not sneaking. I'm light on my feet," Georgia said.

I got a paper towel and wiped up the spill. Then I put the rest of the milk into the bigger bottle, rinsed out the small one, and put it in the bottom of the recycling bin so Mom wouldn't see it.

"Rafe?" Georgia said. "Why are you being so super-weird right now?"

"Trust me," I said. "You don't want to know."

"Yes, I do," Georgia said, because she's nosier than Pinocchio. She likes to know everything.

"Okay, just listen," I said. "But you're not going to like it."

I'm not really sure why I told Georgia about

the soup kitchen. Maybe because my brain was overflowing, and I had to tell *someone*.

"So, that's it," I said. "And whatever you do, don't tell Mom."

"Wow," Georgia said.

"I know. Crazy, right?" I said.

"No," she said. "I mean, you bought all that food just so you could try and fool me with this stupid lie? Way to waste your own time. Not to mention your money."

"I'm not fooling, Georgia," I said.

"Yeah, right," she said. "I don't know what you're up to, but it's not going to work."

Then she took the last pudding cup from the fridge and disappeared again.

Which I guess meant I was on my own for this one.

LiFE VS. RAFe

CHAPTER 29

FIRE WITH FIRE

You know what you need?" Flip said.

"Yeah. A life transplant," I said.

"Nope."

"A WormHole Premium Multi-Platform GameBox."

"No. Well, maybe. But more than that, you need your own personal evil genius," he said.

"Sure," I said. "I'll just run over to the evil genius store and pick one up."

"*Or*," Flip said, "you could look closer to home."

I got his drift. "Ohhh," I said. And then, "*Nooo. There's no way I'm asking my sister for help.*"

We were sitting in the back of the library at school, supposedly doing homework, but mostly talking about my Cheap Walks problem.

"Just think about it," Flip said. "You've got to fight fire with fire, right? And Cheap Walks has *two* evil geniuses."

"Forget it," I said.

"Georgia is definitely a genius," he said. "Besides being pretty cute."

Barf. Whenever he said anything about Georgia being pretty or fun, my ears shriveled up into themselves.

"…And she might even have some good evil ideas," he went on.

"You're right about her being evil," I said. "But asking her to help would be like giving Georgia a free pass into my personal life. And besides—"

But then I stopped. I was about to say, *Besides, she didn't believe me about Grandma at the soup kitchen. Why should she believe me about this?*

Except then I remembered I didn't want to talk about that part. Not even with Flip.

"Besides, what?" Flip asked.

"It doesn't matter," I said. "The point is, I'd rather slow dance with Mrs. Stricker than ask my sister for help. It's not going to happen."

Flip looked like he had more to say, but Mr.

Naguchi was closing in fast with that *ARE YOU WORKING OR AM I KICKING YOU OUT OF THE LIBRARY?* kind of look on his face.

So we switched over to talking about English assignments and social studies reports, ASAP. In middle school, that's what you call survival skills.

Mr. Naguchi gave us a look like we weren't as slick as we thought. Then he turned Flip's workbook right side up.

"Focus, fellas," he said.

After that, we had to stick to doing homework. But it didn't matter. Flip could have thrown in a first-class trip to Hawaii and a gold-plated Jeep, and I still wasn't going anywhere near his idea.

Case closed. Moving on.

CHAPTER 30

PLAN OF ATTACK

The way I saw it was this. The Finn twins were killing me out in the field. And by *in the field,* I mean in the street, where we did our dog-walking.

What I needed was a home-turf advantage. And by *home turf,* I mean Hills Village Middle School.

According to their mom, Eddie and Ethan were going to be brand-new at HVMS that Monday.

If you know me, then you know that I'm pretty much an expert on how to get a detention in that place. Hopefully that meant I'd know a few things about getting someone else a detention. Or even better, *two* someone elses.

I know, I know. Not very mature.

But let me put it this way. If you're in a war

with someone, and you try talking to them, and getting an adult involved, and making a deal... and you STILL wind up with a fistful of dog doo? You're doing something wrong.

Sometimes you have to think outside the box. Even if that's where they keep the rules.

The twins were probably going to be all nervous and distracted on their first day in a new school. I figured that was the perfect time to strike. Now I just had to get ready.

Flip's mom said I could spend Friday AND Saturday night at their house that weekend, which was awesome. It gave us plenty of time to work on our plan, and plenty of time for some TrollQuest too.

So when we weren't storming Prince Xudu's Blood Fortress, or battling giant slugs in the Swamps of Nowhere, we were out buying supplies, and practicing our moves, and getting ready to launch my latest mission.

Welcome to *Operation: Double Down*.

CHAPTER 31

OPERATION: DOUBLE DOWN

When I got to school Monday morning, I had my eyes peeled like a couple of grapes, just waiting to spot Eddie and Ethan and get my plan in motion.

It happened before first period even started, when I was at my locker. But first, Jeanne came up to me.

"Hey, Rafe, do you have the new comic for the school paper?" she asked.

And I thought—*Oops.* "Uh…I kind of forgot to do it over the weekend," I said.

"You did?" she said, like she wasn't exactly surprised, but wasn't exactly happy about it either.

"I was pretty busy," I said.

"Well, can you do it today?" she asked me.

"Uhhhh…" I said, because I couldn't say, "Actually, I'm all booked up executing my new master plan."

"Gosh, Rafe," Jeanne said. "I thought we were working on this paper together. I mean, even if I wanted to, I couldn't do it all by my blergle blargel blarg blarg blarrr…"

Did you notice something there? And I don't mean that Jeanne started speaking Martian. It was more like I lost track of what she was saying.

And when the thing I'm *not* paying attention to is Jeanne Galletta, you know something's up.

Something was. I'd just spotted the twins, and it couldn't have been more perfect. Not only were they right there in the hall, but so was Mrs. Stricker, showing them their lockers and stuff.

So I had to act, super-fast.

"Hey, Jeanne," I said. "If I promise to get you a comic by the end of the day, could I use your phone? Like right now?"

"We're not supposed to use them during school except for emergencies," she said.

"It's a *kind of* emergency," I said. Which was *kind of* the truth.

"Okay," she said, and held it out. "But I want that comic by the end of eighth period."

"Deal," I said, and took the phone. Then I opened my locker and used the door for cover, so I could call Cheap Walks without anyone seeing.

Something told me those guys were *always* open for business. And sure enough, as soon as I dialed the number, I heard a phone ringing down the hall.

Except, it didn't ring. It *barked*.

That's right. Cheap Walks' ring tone sounded like a huge, angry German shepherd. You should have seen the way everyone looked around just then. I think a couple of people dove for cover.

And even better, you should have heard Mrs. Stricker. Her bark is definitely as bad as her bite.

"Cell phone use is NOT allowed during the school day!" she said. "Consider this your first and last warning!"

By now, Jeanne was looking at me like I'd used up all her minutes. But I was done, anyway.

"Okay, thanks, Mom," I said into the phone. "Sorry I, um…left the stove on and the bathtub running like that. See you later!"

Then I handed it back to Jeanne.

"Is everything okay?" Jeanne said.

I looked up the hall one more time. Eddie and Ethan were still shaking in their shoes while Mrs. Stricker walked away. So I guess you could call that the Monday-morning warm-up.

Or maybe more like a *warn*-up, thanks to Mrs. Stricker.

"Yep, everything's just fine," I told Jeanne. "In fact, I think it's going to be a great day."

CHAPTER 32

WHISTLE WHILE YOU WORK

I made my next move between third and fourth period. That's when I tailed Eddie and Ethan through the hall. One of them was carrying his gym stuff, so I could tell they'd be splitting up— which was just what I needed them to do.

As soon as they did, I counted to ten, made sure the coast was clear, and took out my brand-new whistle. It was just like the one Eddie and Ethan used on the street, and I blew it as loud as I could.

Sure enough, those two had each other trained like a couple of circus poodles. As soon as that whistle went off, they both came running to see why the other one had sounded the alarm. And I do mean *running*.

Right up until Mrs. Stricker stopped them in their twin tracks.

"NO RUNNING IN THE HALLS!" she said. "AND WHO BLEW THAT WHISTLE?"

I was listening from around the corner, but I would have paid big bucks to see their faces just then.

"It wasn't me," one of them said.

"It wasn't me," the other said.

"Well, you were *both* running," Mrs. Stricker said. "This is your second warning, and that's as many as you get. Do you understand?"

"Yes, ma'am," they both said.

So far, so good. Unless I completely messed this up, Eddie and Ethan were going to be serving hard time with Sergeant Stricker by the end of their first day.

So after fourth period and before lunch, I dropped two copies of the same note into their lockers, to make double-sure they double-got it.

I knew they wouldn't have the nerve to *not* show up after that. These guys were getting kind of predictable, to tell you the truth.

So during lunch, Flip and I met at my locker and pulled together everything we needed for the big finish—one paper clip, my whistle, an air horn from the sporting goods store, and our nerve. I'd spent fifteen bucks for the air horn and the whistle, but hopefully it would all be worth it.

After that, we split up again. I was going to meet the twins in the bathroom, and Flip was going to wait up the hall for my signal.

I chose the bathroom near the office for a couple of reasons. Nobody ever used it, so we'd have some privacy. But it also meant that when Mrs. Stricker came running again, she wouldn't have very far to go.

Which meant Eddie and Ethan would have somewhere between zero and no chance of getting away. Neither would I, but that was all part of the plan.

Here went nothing!

Or even better, here went a whole lot of *something*.

WHO'S SORRY NOW?

When I got to the bathroom, the twins were already waiting for me.

"What do you want, you dingus?" Eddie said.

"I want to know what your problem is," I said. "You've been coming after me since day one."

"*Our* problem?" Ethan said. "*You* started the whole thing."

"I didn't start anything," I said. "You started it when you tore down my poster at the dog park."

"What are you talking about?" Eddie said. "We never even *saw* your stupid poster. How many times do we have to tell you that?"

"Listen," I said, "I'm just saying, stop messing with my business and I'll stop messing with yours."

"Or else what?" Eddie said.

"Or else find out," I said. Then I held up the whistle. "Last chance. Are we done with this stupid war, or are we just getting started?"

"What a loser," Eddie said. "Come on, Eth. Let's go."

"Don't say I didn't warn you," I told them. Then I gave Flip the signal, which was one long blow on that whistle.

Half a second later, the door popped open and Flip was right there. He held up the air horn and gave it a major-league blast. Then he dropped it on the floor and took off again.

Have you ever heard an air horn before? It sounds like if you took that whistle, multiplied it by infinity, and then turned up the volume.

Plus, with that bathroom echo, I'm pretty sure the whole school heard it. Maybe even *you* heard it, wherever you were.

The twins were smart enough to get moving after that. Which was exactly what I wanted them to do. While all three of us were hustling out the bathroom door, I pulled off my last move.

I'd been thinking about all that magic Mr.

* Earthlings are so loud!
** And delicious, too.

Schneider did, and how he got that quarter to show up in different places. So I'd invented my own version with the whistle and the paper clip, unfolded to make a hook.

All it took was one fast move on our way out of the bathroom. Then by the time we came into the hall, Eddie had that whistle hanging off his back pocket like a piece of evidence at a crime scene.

And of course, Mrs. Stricker got there at the speed of light.

"*WHAT*...WAS...THAT...*NOISE?*" she said.

I had my pinkie in my ear by then, and I gave Ethan a look.

"Hey, warn me next time you're going to do that," I said.

"I didn't do it! You did it!" Ethan said.

"Yeah!" Eddie said.

The air horn was sitting right there on the floor, but unless Mrs. Stricker had a fingerprinting lab in her office, there was no way to prove who had used it.

So then I turned and pointed at Eddie. "Well, if I made that noise," I said, "what's that hanging out of your back pock..."

I kind of trailed off then, because when I pointed at the place where I'd just stuck the whistle, it was gone.

"Do you mean *that?*" Ethan said, and pointed right back at me.

Sure enough, I turned around and that stupid thing was hanging off *my* pocket now. Just like a piece of evidence at a crime scene.

"What a surprise," Mrs. Stricker said. "Let's go,

Rafe. You know the way."

I couldn't believe it. I'd practiced that move with Flip about a hundred times. It was supposed to be foolproof.

But as Mrs. Stricker was marching me to the office, I started to figure out where I went wrong.

See, Flip only has two eyes and two hands. I never practiced on a four-eyed, four-handed monster before. In other words, Cheap Walks had managed to catch me in the act, steal my trick, and trick me right back with it.

Which was genius. *Evil* genius.

Now I was even worse off than when I started. The twins were still out to get me, probably more than ever. I had a brand-new detention. And I was also out fifteen bucks for the supplies.

I don't know what to call that, except maybe a lose-lose-lose situation. And that's a lot of losing.

Even for me.

The one good thing was, I had a new idea for my comic for Jeanne.

CHAPTER 34

FIVE BUCKS' WORTH OF PROOF

I was all out of ideas. Actually, not *all* out. But I was definitely scraping the bottom of the barrel. And when I did, you know what came up?

My sister.

I had to admit it. Flip was right. Georgia had skills that I didn't. And I needed her help, like it or not.

CAUTION! CAUTION!

OPEN ONLY IN EMERGENCY AND EVEN THEN, GOOD LUCK! ('CAUSE YOU'RE GOING TO NEED IT ON THE DOUBLE!)

EVIL GENIUS INSIDE!

So when I got to science class (I still can't really believe we're in the same class, but that's the least of my problems), I sat down right next to her. She looked back at me like I was a B— on her quiz.

"I have to talk to you," I said. "It's important."

"Oh, great," she said. "That means so much to me."

"Actually, I have to show you something. I wasn't lying about Grandma Dotty, and I'm going to prove it to you," I said. "But you have to come with me later today."

"Why would I trust you?" she asked.

I knew all that was coming, so I was ready for her. I handed her half of a five-dollar bill.

"What's this?" she said. "Some kind of joke?"

"It's two dollars and fifty cents," I said.

"It's half a five-dollar bill," she said.

"Then why'd you ask?" I said. "Never mind, don't answer that. The point is, if I'm lying, you can have the other half."

"And if you're *not* lying?"

"Then you give me your half back," I said. "See? I'm *trusting you*."

I know it seems like I'd just broken my number one rule. But it was more like I'd gone from this:

WHEN TO TRUST GEORGIA:

To this:

I needed a win. And to do that, I needed to prove to Georgia how important my dog-walking business was.

And to do *that,* I needed her to see Grandma going into that soup kitchen with her own eyes.

Which is where the five dollars came in. Basically, the only language my sister and I both speak is *money.*

Flash forward to that afternoon, and we're heading over to the church. I'd looked it up online, and they started serving dinner at 4:45. I also knew Grandma Dotty usually got home from her "mah-jongg game" by 5:30. So I had a pretty good idea about when to be there.

"Where are we going?" Georgia kept asking.

"No questions," I said.

"It's freezing out here," she said.

"No complaints either."

"What are we—"

"Shh!" I said, because we were there now. People were already lined up outside, and there was a sign that said PUBLIC MEALS, 4:45–6:00 DAILY.

I cut behind a Dumpster and pulled Georgia back there with me.

"This is stupid. I knew I shouldn't believe you," she said. "You owe me half a five-dollar bill, you big fat liar—"

"Shhhhhhh!" I said, and put a hand over her mouth. Because Grandma had just come around the corner.

"There she is," I said.

Georgia didn't move. She didn't even say anything, which was maybe a first in history. We both just watched while Grandma said hi to the guy with the shopping cart and they both went inside.

"*Now* do you believe me?" I asked her. "That's why I bought all that food for the house. I wasn't making this up."

Georgia still didn't say anything. She was like a statue. Except then this one tear rolled down her cheek.

It's not like I ever *want* Georgia to be sad. It's more like I *want* her to move to Mexico, or get adopted by a family of ferrets. So when I saw her getting all wet around the eyes, I felt guilty.

But in the meantime, business was business. And I still needed to get her on board.

CHAPTER 35

FUNNY BUSINESS

Don't cry," I said. "Your face is going to get
frostbite, and I don't feel like taking you to
the hospital."

"I'm not crying," she said. "My eyes are
watering from the cold."

"Uh-huh," I said.

Then we started walking home, and I explained
the whole thing.

"So now do you see?" I asked her. "We need to
make sure Cheap Walks doesn't drive Dogs To Go
all the way out of business. And we need to do it
soon, because they're on the warpath."

"*We?*" she said.

"I'm not asking for my sake," I said. "I'm asking
for Mom and Grandma. I mean, unless you have

some high-paying job I don't know about."

Georgia didn't say anything to that. But I could tell she was thinking about it.

"So, I just have one question," she said. "If *we* do this, how much money am *I* going to make?"

"Who said anything about that?" I asked. "I already gave you five dollars."

"Okay, well, good luck, then," she said. "Have fun wishing you'd listened to me while you had the chance." She even moved to the other side of the sidewalk.

"Hang on a second," I said.

I knew what was going on. This is the part of running a business they call *negotiation*. Georgia hadn't even dried her eyes and she was right back in evil genius mode. Which I couldn't even complain about because it was what I came to her for in the first place.

Besides, Cheap Walks had two walkers, right? That meant twice the walks and twice the money. Which meant that Georgia could actually pay for herself.

"Okay," I said. "I've thought about it—"

"That was quick," she said.

"Just listen," I said. "I'll cut you in, but you're going to have to walk some dogs."

"No problem," she said.

"And get your own customers too," I said.

"Okay," she said. She was already excited. I could practically see the little dollar signs in her eyes.

"Also, *half* of everything we make goes into the pot for the family," I said.

"That's fair," Georgia said.

"*And* you have to help me deal with Cheap Walks or else the whole thing's off."

"I can do that," she said, like she already had a couple of ideas.

And just like that, I'd bought myself an evil genius. For better or worse.

CHAPTER 36

SECRET SAUCE

We took the long way home. I was in a weirdly good mood, considering I was hanging out with my sister.

But I had another good idea. I made Georgia play along and promise to pay me for part of the operation, starting with that half a five-dollar bill.

"Hey there!" Mom said when we came in. "What brings my favorite customers to Swifty's Diner?"

"I'm buying dinner again," I said. Besides Dave & Buster's, Swifty's was one of my favorite places. Their pie was better than playing TrollQuest. "If it's okay, we'll do some homework while we're here too."

"Of course!" Mom said.

I think she just liked seeing us *not* fight for a while. She also said I didn't have to pay, but I told her I insisted. Swifty let us eat on her discount, anyway, so it was already forty percent off everything.

But all of that was just the smokescreen. The cover. The alibi for the mini-mission—which was the *real* reason we'd come to Swifty's while Mom was working.

We sat at the counter at the far end of the restaurant in Mom's section. From there, I could see all her customers. Which meant I could see when everyone got up.

First, I asked Swifty to make change for me, so I had a pocketful of dollars. Then we ordered the food.

And every time someone got up to leave, we swung into action.

"Hey, Mom, look at this!" Georgia said, and showed her some paper she was working on…

…while I slipped off my stool and pretended to head for the bathroom…

…but made a teeny-tiny detour on the way…

…right past the table where this family had just headed out…

…and I dropped a couple of extra dollars with the tip they left.

Why all the sneaky moves?

Simple.

I knew Mom wouldn't just take the money from us. So this was the only way to give her our extra money without her knowing.

A few minutes later, this older couple got up from the counter and went to pay their bill at the register.

Mom was in the back, and I shoved three bucks into Georgia's hand.

"Go! Now!" I said. "Move, move, move!"

I'm not going to lie. She was even better at this than I was. Someday she's going to make a bundle working for the CIA or the FBI or MI5. In the meantime, she was all over that diner, helping me help Mom work for the T-I-P-S.

"Well, I had a pretty good shift," Mom said, once we were putting on our coats to leave.

"You did?" I asked, all innocent.

"Usually, people get kind of tight right after the holidays, but I guess there's some generous spirit in the air today."

And I looked at Georgia, and she looked at me, and we didn't say a word. But I'm pretty sure we were thinking the same thing.

Mission accomplished.

CHAPTER 37

CHEAT WALKS

It didn't take long for Georgia to start earning her keep in the dog-walking business either. She had two new customers by Sunday afternoon, and that wasn't even the best part.

When she knocked on my door and came into my room that day, there was this *look* in her eyes. It reminded me of one of those nature documentaries, where you see a lion just before she eats an antelope.

"What is it?" I said.

"I have some big news," she said.

That got my attention. "About Cheap Walks?"

"Yeah," she said. "You're never going to believe this, but they're *cheating*."

For a second, I got excited. But then I got

confused. "Hang on," I said. "How do you cheat at dog-walking?"

"By *not* walking the dogs," she said. "Here— look!"

Then she opened her laptop on my desk to show me some pictures.

"So what does this mean?" I said.

"It *means* they're lying to their customers!" Georgia said. "Duh! Everyone's paying for their dogs to get fresh air and sunshine, not sit around someone's garage and wait for a turn on a stupid treadmill."

"How did you even get those pictures?" I said. "It's only been two days."

"You think *they* take weekends off?" she said. "Seriously, Rafe. You need to up your game."

Georgia was definitely onto something, but there was just one other problem here. I told Mom a long time ago that I wasn't going to do any more spying with cameras. Believe it or not, I've already been there, done that, and gotten into big trouble for it.

"I can't use those pictures," I said. "I promised Mom I wouldn't do this kind of thing—"

"Yeah, but *you* didn't take the pictures," Georgia said. "I did. And besides, even if you can't use them, Eddie and Ethan don't know that. They just have to *think* you will."

And I thought—*wow*. My sister was even better at this stuff than I thought.

"Yeah, okay," I said. "I'll talk to them tomorrow."

"Wrong again," Georgia said. "They're going to be all over you tomorrow. You have to do this now. And I'm coming with you."

"That's not going to happen," I said.

"Okay, fine," she said, and closed her laptop. "I guess you could just *describe* the pictures to them when you get there. Because if I'm staying home, so is my computer."

I was starting to think I'd created some kind of monster. But you know what else? Monsters can be pretty useful if you use them the right way.

So we put on our coats and told Mom we were taking Junior out for a walk.

"It's so nice to see you two doing things together," Mom said.

"I know, right?" Georgia said, giving me this big smile—the same kind you might see on a lion just before she takes her first bite of antelope.

CHAPTER 38

FAKE IT TILL YOU MAKE IT

So I hightailed it over to the Finns' house with Junior and Tagalong Khatchadorian (also known as Georgia). She was right, though. I didn't have any time to lose. Monday morning, I'd see the twins in school. And Monday afternoon, I'd be back out walking my customers, which was when they'd probably try to hit me again.

"Hi, Mrs. Finn," I said when she answered the door. "Are Eddie and Ethan home?"

"Come in," she said. "The boys are in the garage."

"Oh, *are* they?" Georgia said, like she was in a movie or something.

"I'll just go get them," Mrs. Finn said.

"Actually," I told her, "we can talk to them out there. It'll only take a second."

So she led us back through the kitchen and out to the garage. Sure enough, the twins were there, along with a bunch of junk, a big workbench, and one beat-up old treadmill.

"Boys? You have some visitors," Mrs. Finn said.

I was kind of hoping to catch them in the act, but they were just fooling around with some tools.

"What are you doing here?" Eddie asked.

"Be polite, please," Mrs. Finn said, and then closed the door.

"Nice treadmill," I said.

"Is that why you came over? To talk about exercise equipment?" Eddie asked.

"Actually, yeah," I said. "Because I was just wondering what your customers might think of *these*."

I looked down at Georgia and she set her laptop on the workbench. Then she opened it up, really slowly, like it had explosives inside or something. I think she just liked the attention.

Then she pulled up a picture of someone's cocker spaniel tied right to the treadmill and stood back so they could see.

"Looks a little dangerous to me," Georgia said.

"For the dogs, I mean. But maybe...well...maybe for you guys too."

Eddie and Ethan looked at each other like they were cornered. Which they basically were.

"Who are *you?*" Eddie demanded.

Georgia smiled in her smug little way. "Rafe's sister, and the new co-president of Dogs to Go. Nice to meet you."

"So listen," I said. "I'm seriously ready to put all of this behind us. I wouldn't even *think* about sending those pictures out to your customers."

Now they looked a little bit confused, and a little bit relieved.

"But *I* would," Georgia said, and the twins looked a tiny bit *less* relieved.

Then Georgia kept going. "What my brother's trying to say is, you messed with the wrong family. You got caught. And now we're offering you a way out of this. See? You leave our business alone—"

"And we leave you alone," I said, because now she was doing all the talking and getting all the best lines.

"I guess we have to think about that," Eddie said.

"Nope," I said. "The offer expires as soon as we walk out that door."

"Take it or leave it," Georgia said.

"Yeah, I just said that," I said.

Eddie and Ethan looked at each other again, for a long time. Maybe they had some silent twin language, for all I know. Because then Eddie nodded.

"Yeah, okay," he said. "Deal."

"What you do is your business," I said. "What I do is my business—"

"*Our* business," Georgia said.

"And let's just leave each other alone from now on," I said.

We didn't bother shaking on it, but I had a good feeling about this. Now that we had something on them, they had a reason to back off once and for all.

Thirty seconds later, we were outside and headed home with Junior. And just like that, the war was over. *Amazing*.

"*Soooo?*" Georgia said, once we were heading back up the street.

"What?" I said.

"Oh, come on!" she said. "I just saved your butt, big-time."

"Yeah, that could have gone worse," I said. Which was as close to a compliment as she was going to get. Georgia's head was already big enough.

And besides, she barely took a breath before she was onto the next thing.

"Okay, well, good, because I had a few ideas about how we can make Dogs To Go even better," she said. "And hopefully make more money too."

"I'm listening," I said.

And the funny thing is, I really was.

CHAPTER 39

CHA-CHING II: THE SEQUEL

It's baaa-aaaaaack! Can you hear that sound?

Cha-ching!

Cha-ching!

Because instead of looking over my shoulder for the next sabotage all the time, I was looking ahead to my next five bucks, and the next, and the next. Now that the war was over, Cheap Walks was leaving Dogs To Go alone, and we were growing my business as much as we could.

Well, okay. *Our* business.

Besides her promising future in global espionage, it turned out Georgia was good at coming up with ideas too. And I was pretty good at making them happen.

Like for instance, our next invention, which I

like to call the Walking Billboard. Every customer who let us use it got a discount. And believe me, those discounts paid for themselves, because this thing was impossible to miss.

In other words—cha-ching!

Pretty soon, we had five more new customers, a fleet of company vehicles, a lifetime supply of Zoom and M&M's in the garage, and a six-figure book deal for Junior to tell his story, *Walking Is*

Winning: The Junior Khatchadorian Story.

Well, five new customers, anyway, with all kinds of good stuff still to come—fingers crossed. So after a private consult with my corporate vice-presidents, I agreed to let Georgia start coming to our staff meetings.

And by staff meetings, I mean Flip and I would play TrollQuest in his basement, and Georgia would throw out all kinds of new ideas. Like for instance—

"We should set up a table at the school winter carnival!" she said at the next meeting. "Everyone's going to be there, including a ton of parents. And they're the ones who hire dog-walkers."

"Hmm," I said, while I fit another key in the door of the stone tower I was trying to open. The giant slugs were back, and I was all out of salt grenades to fight them with. I had to hurry. "What do you think, Flip?"

"I'm in," he said. I thought he was talking about the tower, but he wasn't. "The only thing is, who's going to care about dog-walking at a carnival?"

"Then we have to make them care," I said.

"Ooh! Ooh!" Georgia said like there was electric current in her chair. "What about free dog biscuits?"

"Yawn," Flip said, just before he threw his last vial of fighting potion at the tower door and blew the whole thing away in a cloud of green smoke.

Which gave me my next idea.

"You know what?" I said. "I've got this. I'll take it from here."

Who says video games don't have anything to teach you? Because I'd just gotten the brainstorm I needed, and unless Cheap Walks had...oh, I don't know...MAGIC POWERS...they were never going to top what I had in mind.

Now I just had to make the magic happen.

CHAPTER 40

SPECIAL REQUEST

On the way home from Flip's, I ditched Georgia and went straight over to Mr. Schneider's house. This one was my idea, and I wanted to see it through myself.

"Come in, come in, my friend," Mr. Schneider said. "But tell me I'm not crazy. Didn't Maxie already get his walk today?"

"Actually, I wanted to ask you a favor," I said. "Maybe a big one."

"How big?" he said. "Three hundred pounds? Four hundred pounds?"

Mr. Schneider was pretty hokey, but here's the thing. The more I got to know him, the funnier he seemed.

"I need a magician," I said.

"Ah," he said. "Well, you came to the right place."

"Actually, it's for my table at the school carnival on Friday night," I said. "I was kind of hoping you might come and—"

"Hold it right there, Rafe," Mr. Schneider said. "I don't know about that. Magic is all bang, flash, and boom these days. Trust me, nobody's interested in an old-school guy like me anymore."

"Sure they are," I said. "You're really good. Georgia and Flip think so too. I mean, the HVMS carnival isn't exactly the big time, but you'd kind of be the star attraction."

Mr. Schneider thought about it for a minute. Like for an actual minute. I was starting to wonder if maybe he'd forgotten what we were talking about, when he finally spoke up again.

"You know, it's been a long time since anyone asked for Magic Murray," he said. "But what the heck? I guess I could dust off the old tux."

"Awesome!" I said. "Just tell me what you need."

Now I was more excited about the carnival than ever. And I think Mr. Schneider was happy about it too. Because when I was getting ready to leave, he kind of turned away from me and pulled this handkerchief out of his sleeve—and then another, and another, and another, and another, and another…

…and then he wiped a little tear out of his eye.

That was when I knew I'd done the right thing for *someone* that day. Which felt really good. Also, I was ready to finally kick some Cheap Walks butt.

Once and for all.

And fair and square.

SPLORT!

So everything was going great, right?

Right!

And that meant everything was just going to *keep* going that way, right?

Well...

If you thought so, you probably haven't ever met me before.

There I was, sitting in my room a couple of days later, when Georgia came cruising in without even knocking.

"Hello?" I said. "Learn to knock. It's good for your health."

"Yeah, yeah, yeah," she said. "Trust me, you need to see this."

Then she closed the door and locked it, and

then checked the lock, like she was sitting on big government secrets or something.

"This better be interesting," I said.

"I guess *interesting* is one word for it," she said. "But if I was going to pick three words, it would be more like *really bad news*."

And all I could think was—*It was nice while it lasted.*

"See, I did some more research," she said.

"Of course you did," I said.

"I figured it would be good to go all the way back, and make sure...Well, let me just show you," she whispered.

Then she opened her laptop again. This time, instead of pictures, she had a video. It was all grainy and black-and-white.

"Is that from a security camera?" I asked.

"Yep," she said.

I recognized the dog park right away. You could see the gate, the fence, the trees, the bulletin board—everything. I could even see Candy Crush playing around with her little poodle, Beckham.

"Where'd you get this?" I asked.

"Abigail Schultz's dad works at the doughnut shop across from the park, and they have a security camera on the building," Georgia said. "I'm not really friends with Abigail, but *her* best friend is Martha Brewer, and—"

"Never mind," I said. "Just get to the point."

"Hang on," she said. "It's coming right up at…"

She actually took out a little pad of notes and looked at it.

"Four thirty-five and eighteen seconds," she said.

Seriously, my sister was born to spy.

And sure enough, at exactly four thirty-five and eighteen seconds, something happened on the screen. Candy Crush's dog took a squat.

"There!" Georgia said.

"*That's* what you wanted me to see?" I asked.

"News flash, I walk dogs. I see that every day."

"Just watch," Georgia said.

Candy Crush reached into her pocket and came up empty. She looked around. Then she walked over to the bulletin board.

And *then* she tore down my poster. Not only that, but she used it to clean up Beckham's poop and threw the whole thing in the trash.

"No way!" I said.

"Hold on. There's more," Georgia said.

She fast-forwarded the video a bunch of minutes, until one of the twins showed up. It was too grainy to see if it was Eddie or Ethan. Whoever it was, he put a new poster up in the one blank spot left on the board—where mine used to be.

I couldn't believe it.

"You mean—" I said.

"Yeee-ah," Georgia said, really slowly, like my brain might explode if I got too much bad news too fast.

"So they never—"

"Nope," she said.

"And I, uh—"

"Mm-hmmm," she said.

In other words, the Finn twins weren't lying. They *didn't* take my poster. And I really did start that war.

Which meant I was going to have to come clean with Cheap Walks.

And...apologize?

And *that's* right about when my brain exploded anyway.

CHAPTER 42

THIS IS GETTING OLD

I probably don't have to tell you this, but sometimes growing up and acting more mature is about as much fun as a permanent detention.

When I was little, my problems were things like what kind of cereal I could get Mom to buy, or how to draw hands and feet that didn't look like balloons.

Now I was trying to come up with a way to tell Eddie and Ethan the truth, and maybe even (barf) tell them I was sorry.

I know, I know. Me, doing the right thing without an adult forcing me to? *Crazy Town.* Maybe I did start that war, but those guys weren't exactly goody-goodies. It's not like they deserved...

well...*anything* from me.

But at the same time, if all this was my fault, and I *didn't* say something, how was I any better than them?

The old Rafe never would have even wondered about that kind of stuff. But I'm not the old Rafe anymore. I'm more like Rafe 2.0. And there's no going back.

But wait. What if I confessed and they told their mom, who would tell *my* mom what I did? She might make me shut down Dogs To Go...and that would mean the end of my WormHole dreams forever.

And more importantly, I couldn't help out the family anymore.

I knew Mom pretty well, though (practically my whole life), and deep down, I figured she would want me to do the right thing. Even if it was the *worst* thing.

I decided to make like a Band-Aid bandit and pull the whole thing off fast before I could think about it too much.

I took a deep breath. I wished I was somewhere else.

Then I picked up the phone and dialed Cheap Walks' number.

"Hello, Cheap Walks!" one of them said.

"Is this Eddie? Or Ethan?" I said.

"Ethan speaking, how may I help you?" he said.

"This is Rafe," I said. "And I—"

That's when I got the world's loudest *CLICK*.

"Hello?"

Of course, he was already gone. But I wasn't giving up that easily.

So I tried again the next day at school. In fact, I tried a bunch of times—at their lockers, in gym, and once when I saw Eddie in the hall alone.

And every time I got anywhere near either of those twins, it was like we were two magnets facing the wrong way. They'd just go flying off in some other direction.

I even tried putting it in writing. Then I went by their table at lunch, dropped the note between them where they couldn't miss it, and kept on walking.

A second later, I heard a crumpling sound behind me. Then that note flew right past my head and landed in the garbage can for two points.

Now I was getting kind of ticked off. Because I realized something else. These guys weren't just avoiding me. They were *competing* with me. At *everything*.

I guess that would have been a good time to just let the whole thing go. But do you remember earlier when I told you how sometimes I take things a little too far? Or a lot too far?

And how when I get mad, my brain goes kind of *kerflooey*?

And how sometimes (okay, a lot of the time), I just can't keep my stupid mouth shut?

Well, I do, and it does, and I can't.

In other words, I thought, *Challenge accepted.* I was going to do whatever it took to *make* these guys listen.

Whether any of us were going to like it or not.

BiG NiGHT

Finally, the night of the carnival came. It was pretty awesome, I have to admit. They had games and food all set up in the cafeteria. The school band was playing on the stage in the gym. And right there on the gym floor, anyone who wanted to could set up a table.

That's where we were, along with the PTA, the chess club, some seventh graders' babysitting business, and a whole ton of others.

But no Cheap Walks. I guess they didn't think of it, which was fine with me.

Meanwhile, nobody had a bigger crowd at their table than Dogs To Go! Magic Murray was a gigantic hit. He was doing the quarter trick, the handcuff trick, fancy card shuffling, and a bunch of magic I'd never seen, while half of Hills Village stopped, and watched, and even signed up for some dog-walking.

It was almost like we had *too many* good ideas. Junior was there, saying hi to people and getting petted like crazy. We also had homemade dog biscuits from Grandma Dotty to give away. And I drew the T-shirt designs myself.

"Step right up! Check it out!" Flip kept saying. Georgia was signing up customers. And I helped Magic Murray with his props and stuff.

I felt like I was at the Las Vegas Middle School carnival instead of Hills Village. It was all going exactly like we planned.

Right up until Eddie and Ethan showed up at our table. I think they were just looking at the magic. Maybe they didn't even know it was me at first. Not until they were standing right there, and we were face-to-face, with nothing but a folding table between us.

The timing was terrible. Couldn't have been worse. But you know me. I went for it anyway.

"Listen," I said before they could make themselves disappear. "I've been trying to tell you guys something all week. I just want to talk. What's your big problem?"

Then Eddie leaned right in and got in my face, right in front of everyone.

"You don't get it, do you?" he said. "We're not interested in anything you have to say."

"And here's a news flash, Einstein," Ethan said. "You can't *make* us listen."

And I thought—*Oh, really?*

That's when I picked up Magic Murray's magic handcuffs, reached out, and—*CLICK!*—popped one

of the cuffs around Eddie's wrist, right before—
CLICK!—I popped the other cuff on myself.

Now we were going to have that talk.

And at least one of them was going to listen.

CHAPTER 44

UNNECESSARY CUFF-NESS

It wasn't exactly a plan. It just kind of happened. And now that I was attached at the wrist to half of Cheap Walks, I had to go with it.

"*What are you doing?*" Eddie yelped.

"I'm coming clean," I said.

"That's what you think!" Ethan said, and yanked on Eddie so hard, I slid halfway across the table.

"Hey! Let go of him!" Flip said.

"I *can't!*" Eddie said.

"Not you. The other one!" Flip said. Then he grabbed my arm and yanked me back. Right before Ethan pulled Eddie even harder in the other direction. It was like a full-on tug-of-war, except Eddie and I were the rope.

And I think my arm had just grown a foot too.

"Eddie…just…listen…to…me…" I kind of grunted out.

"Why…should…I?" he grunted back. Flip was pretty strong, but so was Ethan. It was like a tie, and we weren't going anywhere.

"Because…" I said.

"'Cause…why?" Eddie said.

"Get off him!" Flip yelled.

"You first!" Ethan yelled.

"Because this war…was…*all…my fault!*" I said.

And that stopped Eddie cold—but not Flip. He was still pulling like crazy, which meant Eddie came flying at me, right across that table. The whole thing fell over. Dog biscuits and playing cards went flying everywhere. And Eddie and I kept on going. In fact, the two of us didn't stop until we'd plowed right into the Babysitters' Club table and sent all of their stuff flying too.

I guess you could say we had the whole gym's attention now. Even the band stopped playing. And I could see Sergeant Stricker coming in hot too.

"Where on earth did those handcuffs come from?" Mrs. Stricker said, practically skidding to a stop next to us.

"Rafe?" Mr. Schneider said, looking at the cuffs, then at me.

"Sorry," I said. "I had to borrow them."

"Well, now you can...un-borrow them!" Mrs. Stricker said.

"I don't have a key," I said.

"What?" she said.

"They're magic cuffs," I said. "Only Magic Murray knows how to open them."

"No, I don't," Mr. Schneider said.

"**WHAT???**" everyone said, including me.

"Just kidding," he said. "Stand back, everyone. I'll have those off in a jiff."

"Actually—" I said.

And he stopped and looked at me.

"I just need one minute," I told him.

"Excuse me!" Mrs. Stricker said. "Mr. Murray, is it?"

"You can call me Magic Murray," Mr. Schneider said.

"Yes, well...Mr....Magic...or whoever you are,"

Mrs. Stricker said. "Can you please free these boys from each other? Immediately?"

Mr. Schneider looked at me. Then he looked at Mrs. Stricker.

"Yes to the first part," Mr. Schneider said. "But not so much on the *immediately*."

"What is THAT supposed to mean?" Mrs. Stricker asked him.

I couldn't tell who was madder—her, Eddie, or Ethan. Flip was totally loving it.

"Let's just say I owe Rafe," Mr. Schneider said. "He's a very nice boy. A good boy. And if he says he needs a minute to sort things out with this other fine young man, I'm going to give him the benefit of the doubt. Go ahead, Rafe."

"We'll see about that!" Mrs. Stricker said. Then she started pushing her way back through the crowd and disappeared.

For the moment, anyway.

"Just give me one minute to explain," I told Eddie.

He looked around like he didn't have a choice. Which he didn't. At least not until Mrs. Stricker could dig up the bolt cutters, or the dynamite, or whatever she was probably looking for right now.

In other words, the clock was ticking, and I had to talk fast.

CHAPTER 45

COMING CLEAN(iSH)

All those times I thought about coming clean with Cheap Walks, I never really imagined it in the middle of the HVMS gym with about half the town listening in.

But then again, I never imagined a lot of things.

So I made it as short and sweet as possible. Or at least short, anyway. And I told them everything you already know about what happened.

"So you've been lying all this time?" Ethan asked when I was done.

"No," I said. "I just found out about it."

"*I* found out about it first!" Georgia butted in, because there's nothing she likes better than extra credit.

"So, yeah," I said. "That's kind of it."

Now that I'd said it, I wasn't really sure what was supposed to happen next. But Mrs. Stricker sure was.

"HERE WE ARE! HERE WE ARE! MAKE ROOM! COMING THROUGH!" she said. And right behind her, I could see Mr. Mint, the custodian. I could also see the giant bolt cutters in his hand.

So I turned to face Mr. Schneider. At least, I tried to, but it wasn't easy with Eddie squirming around like a worm on a hook.

"I guess I'm out of time," I told Magic Murray. "You don't want to lose your cuffs."

"What do you say, son?" Mr. Schneider said to Eddie. "Sounds to me like a big misunderstanding. How about we all just forgive and forget?"

"Yeah, *right*," Eddie said.

In other words—no way.

And that was pretty much all we had time for.

"Excuse me!" Mrs. Stricker said. They were practically on top of us now. Eddie was yanking my arm off, trying to hold the cuffs up for Mr. Mint to cut.

But Magic Murray kept his cool. Not to mention his style.

"Everyone stand back!" he told the crowd. Then he waved his hands over the cuffs three times. "Dallas, Springfield, Kalamazoo!" he said, just before they dropped off and right into his palm for a clean catch.

Not bad. People even applauded.

And Magic Murray took a little bow. Which was like the end of the show.

In fact, it was like the end of a lot of things.

CHAPTER 46

SHUTTING IT DOWN

I've never been sent to the principal's office on a Friday night before. I guess there's a first time for everything.

I also think we set some kind of record for the most number of people in there, with me, Flip, Eddie, Ethan, Mrs. Stricker, Georgia, Mr. Schneider, and even Junior—plus Mom and Mrs. Finn, who both got called in.

"Clearly, there is a problem outside of the school that's become a problem inside the school," Mrs. Stricker said. I could only see part of her from where I was kind of wedged in there. But that was plenty enough for me.

"Well, it won't be a problem any longer," Mom said. She and Mrs. Finn had been talking, and

they looked like they had something to say.

"I'm listening," Mrs. Stricker said.

"There won't be any more trouble between these two dog-walking businesses," Mrs. Finn said, "because we're putting them both out of operation."

"NOOOO!" Eddie, Ethan, and I all said it at the same time, like we were triplets or something.

"You heard her," Mom said. "Maybe this was my fault—"

"*Our* fault," Mrs. Finn said. "We shouldn't have let it go this far. But we warned you boys about this."

"Honestly, we were hoping you could be mature enough to work it out," Mom said. "I guess we were wrong."

I didn't know what to say. Actually, scratch that. It was more like I knew exactly what to say. I just kind of wished I didn't have to.

But this was the new Rafe. The older, more mature, big-pain-in-my-own-butt Rafe, who never knew when to shut up.

"Put me out of business," I said. "Not them."

"Excuse me?" Mrs. Finn said.

Eddie and Ethan were looking at me like I was just as insane as they thought all along. But I kept going.

"None of this would have happened if it wasn't for me," I told everyone.

And of course then I had to tell the whole embarrassing story all over again, including how Candy Crush had used my poster as a poop scoop, and how I thought Eddie or Ethan had torn it down.

"So if anyone started that war, it was me," I said.

Mrs. Stricker smiled like she'd known it all along.

"Well, that's the thing about wars," Mrs. Finn said. "Usually, everyone loses." Then she looked at the twins. "We'll talk more about this when we get home."

Mom gave me a look that pretty much said— *Ditto*.

"I hope they're not so grounded that they can't come back here this weekend," Mrs. Stricker said. "Someone has to clean up the mess they've made of my gymnasium."

Of course, we weren't *that* grounded. I wish. So on top of everything else, I was going to spend my whole weekend with Mrs. Stricker, Eddie, and Ethan. It was like the World Series of GET ME OUT OF HERE.

And just for the record…

You might have noticed something about what I *didn't* say in there. I mean, I told the truth, for sure, but I never did apologize to the twins. I just couldn't do it. Not to them.

Maybe that would have been the extra-deluxe, *really* grown-up thing to do, but give me a break. Nobody grows up overnight. Especially me.

I guess I'm more like a work in progress.

CHAPTER 47

GROUP HUG

By the time we got home, I was starting to think I'd made a huge mistake. Like maybe I'd done the *wrong* right thing, taking responsibility like that. Maybe I should have tried harder to keep my dog-walking business.

But it was too late now. I know, because I asked Mom at the end of the looooong talk we had at the kitchen table.

"Absolutely not," Mom said. "You really blew this one, Rafe. I'm glad you owned up to it in Mrs. Stricker's office, but that was too little, too late."

"I'll take it over!" Georgia said, coming into the kitchen. "I'm way more responsible. Ooh! Maybe I'll give it a new name! What if I call it—"

"No, sweetie," Mom said. "Let's just let this go."

That's when it really started to hit me. Dogs To Go wasn't just about me, remember. It was also about helping the family. And now I wouldn't able to do that anymore.

"But you don't understand," I said.

"Please?" Georgia said. She and I kept looking at each other, but there wasn't anything we could say in front of Mom.

"Is something going on that I don't know?" Mom asked. "What's with the big stares?"

"It's nothing," I said. "We just really wanted to keep going, because…well, because…"

"Because we're so poor!" Georgia blurted out.

"*Georgia!*" I shouted. Seriously, if any human being could use an Off switch, it's my sister.

"It's not like she doesn't already know!" Georgia said.

"What are you two talking about?" Mom said. "Listen, we're never going to be rich, but we're okay."

"Then why is Grandma eating at the soup kitchen?" I asked. There was no sense holding back now.

Mom stopped and squinted at me. "How do you

know about that?" she said. That's when Grandma Dotty muted the TV. A second later, she came in and sat down with us.

"I wasn't spying," I told Grandma. "I saw you going in there. And then I went back with Georgia and we saw you going in again. So we kind of put two and two together."

Mom looked at both of us. Then she reached out and took one of my hands and one of Georgia's too.

"We didn't want you to worry, because you don't have to," Mom said. "Some families just need a little help, including us. But it's nothing to be ashamed of."

"In fact, I volunteer every other day," Grandma said. "Right after my mah-jongg game. Some days I eat, some days I work. That way, I feel like I'm earning my soup."

It was all making more sense now. In the best possible way.

"Well, we still have some money for you," Georgia said. "Don't we, Rafe?"

"We've been saving up," I said. Then I went to get the shoe box out of my drawer.

When I showed Mom the $265 we'd saved ($50

from Georgia, $215 from me), she looked like she was totally touched. It was like she wanted to cry and laugh at the same time.

"This is *so* sweet," Mom said. She already had us both by the hand, and now she pulled us all into one of her big group hugs.

"Listen, kids," Mom said. "That's your money. I really appreciate the thought, but I want you to keep it."

She didn't have to ask Georgia twice. It took about five seconds for her to count out her fifty bucks and take it back.

That left me $215. Plus the $175 I had in the bank. Which was *almost* enough for a WormHole Premium system, I realized.

"Hey, Georgia," I said. "Can I borrow nine dollars?"

"Get your own," she said. "Now that we're out of business, I don't know if you'll ever pay me back."

But then she looked over at Mom, and Mom didn't even have to say a word.

"Okay, *fii-inne*," Georgia said. Then she pulled out her money and chose the wrinkliest ten-dollar bill she had.

"Thanks," I said. I started to take it, but she held it back.

"Where's my change?" she said, and waited for me to hand her a one-dollar bill. And sign an IOU. And promise to pay her back, just as soon as I figured out how to make some money again.

So I guess you could say things were getting back to normal. Which you might think is where the happy-ending part of this story could start up.

But you'd be wrong.

There was still another whole war to fight.

CHAPTER 48

STINKER AND GEO

I never expected to find myself here with this wide-eyed troll girl, fighting my way through the Maze of the Mist for the second time. I thought I'd conquered this thing already.

But here we are. I know we're going to have to navigate the whole thing backward after we pick up the invisible lantern from the molten iron pool at the center of the maze. But I don't tell that to Geo. She can figure it out for herself.

Her eyes are about three times the size of mine. You'd think she'd notice a few of the clues along the way, like the tiny markers cut into the walls that she keeps running right past.

Oh well. I'm not here to make sure she gets out alive. That's *her* job.

"You sure you want to go this way?" I say.

"I don't get it. We've tried every path there is—"

That's when she steps on a trigger stone and opens one of the hidden panels. But not the good kind. Before you can say "Gulp!" we're facing down a giant ratzard. It's half rat, half lizard, and about the size of a sports car.

And let's just say ratzards are *not* picky eaters.

"Do I use my sword?" Geo asks me.

"What do you think?" I say.

"I'm going to use my sword," she says.

But that's only because she doesn't know ratzards have an IQ of about 200. They may look

like ugly pink-eyed rodents with long green tails,
but they've got the brains of an Einstein. And
they can smell aggression too. One whiff, and they
strike.

I take a step back, because I know what's about
to happen. Before Geo can even get her blade free,
she's halfway down that monster's throat and on
her way to its stomach.

Game over!

"AUGHHH!" Georgia shouted, and sat back on
the couch. "Why didn't you warn me?"

"How are you ever going to learn if I tell you
everything?" I asked her.

She looked like she wanted to throw her
controller across the room, but I knew she
wouldn't. She spent thirty-nine dollars of her own
money on it.

See, after spending an awkwardly silent
weekend cleaning up the gym with the Twin
Terrors (if you thought I'd end up being best
buds with them after this whole nutty war, you
thought way wrong), I went and *finally* bought the
WormHole Premium Multi-Platform GameBox! I'd
been letting Georgia play TrollQuest with me for

the low, low price of one dollar an hour.

"I'm never going to get out of that maze," she said. "Just give me a clue."

"No problem," I said. "Clues are fifty cents apiece. Or you can spring for the mega-clue, but that's two-fifty."

"MOM!" Georgia shouted. "Rafe's blackmailing me! Again!"

"That's a dollar!" Mom said.

Anytime we argued with each other now, it had a price attached. And mostly, it was working. My mom's kind of a genius in her own way, if you ask me. Since Dogs To Go is officially shut down, handing over a dollar just to scream at Georgia is way too expensive.

But here's a little secret for you. I actually *like* playing TrollQuest with Georgia, and I don't just mean for the money.

The truth is, she's always going to kick my butt when it comes to school. So at least I have this. It's not what you'd call an even trade, but it's something, anyway. She has school, I have video games. I don't even know if that means you should be glad for me, or feel sorry for me, or what.

But you know what else? I can't spend my time worrying about that right now. I've got things to do. My own dog to walk. Comics to draw.

And quests to quest.

CHAPTER 49

MAGIC MURRAY RIDES AGAIN

Knock-knock-knock!

I opened the door and leaned inside Magic Murray's dressing room. Which was really just a public bathroom.

"You almost ready, M.M.?" I asked him. "The crowd's getting restless."

Mr. Schneider looked in the mirror and took off his hat. Then he put it back on again. Then he adjusted it, just so.

"Is everything set onstage?" he asked me.

"All good to go," I said. "Now they just need you."

"Well then, let's give them what they want," he said, and headed out of the bathroom.

"Good luck!" I told him.

"No, no, no," he said. "You don't say 'Good luck.' You say 'Break a leg.' Or maybe with me, it's more like 'Break a hip.' Ba-dum-bum! Are you writing these down?"

He was kidding, though. I was finally figuring out Mr. Schneider's sense of humor.

And I was learning all this stuff about showbiz, too. Like how to get some "gigs" for Magic Murray. He was calling himself "the world's oldest magician" now. I don't know if that was technically true, but it got the people at the soup kitchen interested, anyway.

And who knows? Maybe pretty soon, I'll start finding more places for him to perform. Maybe even places that pay real money, and not just free dinner. And maybe…just maybe…after that, I can start earning some commissions.

Hey, what can I say? I like making money. Who doesn't?

But I like working with Mr. Schneider too. He says I'm the best thing to happen to his career since the night Freddy "Fast Fingers" DaSilva got arrested and couldn't go onstage. Someday, I'll get him to tell me that whole story. He says he's got a million of them.

In the meantime, just sit back, relax, and enjoy the show. I know I will!

Pies donated by:
Swifty's Diner

Isaiah is a special mouse—
he can talk and laugh and read, just like you!
And he'll do anything to find his missing
ninety-six brothers and sisters.
Even if it means dealing with cats, hawks,
and the biggest danger of all…
humans!

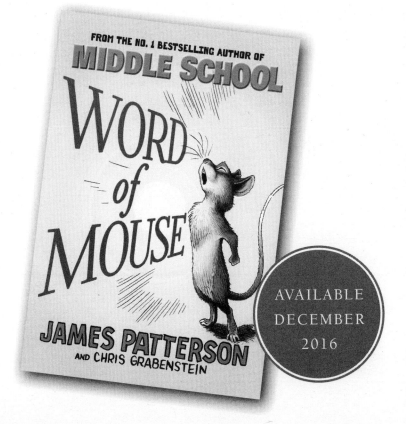

FROM THE NO. 1 BESTSELLING AUTHOR OF
MIDDLE SCHOOL
WORD of MOUSE
JAMES PATTERSON
and CHRIS GRABENSTEIN

AVAILABLE
DECEMBER
2016

CHAPTER 1

*"The world is always biggest
when you're small."*
—Isaiah

My story starts on the day I lost my entire family.
I'm running as fast as I can behind my big
brothers and sisters. Down the hall. Past the mop
bucket. Toward the open door.

We're escaping from a place that's foul and creepy
and 100 percent HORRIBLE!

It's also the only home my family and I have ever
known.

My brothers and sisters are leading the way to our
freedom. All ninety-six of 'em. I'm the youngest, not
to mention the smallest. All I have to do is tail after
them, just like I always do. Wherever they lead, I will

follow. I know it'll be a safer place. And better. It has to be!

Abe says so. Winnie, too.

We squeeze through that tiny crack between the door and the wall and enter the Land of the Giants.

Outside.

The place none of us has ever been before.

Have I mentioned how terrified I am?

Oh, no!

A lumpy black mountain reeking of rancid vegetables blocks our way forward. It forces my family to split up. To scatter in all directions.

"You guys?" I cry. "Wait up!"

They can't wait. It's too dangerous.

I try taking a shortcut to catch up with them. I run *over* the mountain.

Bad idea.

My right rear paw punches through something as thin as an eggshell. My leg plunges down into a slimy hole, and I can't lift it out. This isn't a mountain. It's a big, black plastic sack filled with garbage.

"You guys?"

My brothers and sisters have totally disappeared.

And I'm trapped.

So, I do what I always do. I panic.

"HELP!" I yell.

This escape was my big brother Benji's idea. But Benji's gone. So are Abe and Winnie and—

I hear the heavy thuds of human shoes behind me. Someone's coming.

I yank at my leg. It won't budge. I yank again.

On the third yank, I finally tug my foot free. I need to run. I need to find my family. Because without them, I don't have any idea where I'm supposed to go or what I'm supposed to do!

On the other side of the garbage mountain, I skirt around a crumpled bag labeled D-O-R-I-T-O-S and reach a ledge.

"Winnie? Abe?"

I look around. Can't see anybody.

Then I look down.

There's a three-foot drop to a steel grate covering a dark tunnel.

I close my eyes tight and leap.

I land with a splash in cold, scummy water. I hate when my feet get wet.

"You guys?" I call out. "Did anybody else take the sewer drain? Anybody? Hello?"

No answer. Not even a squeak. Just my own voice echoing back at me.

I've heard humans say, "Are you a man, or are you a mouse?" when one of them is afraid and the other one needs him to be brave.

Well, I am definitely a mouse.

My name is Isaiah. I have never been more frightened in my whole life, and that's saying something, because my whole life has been one big fright fest. But it doesn't get any worse than this.

I don't know where I am. And I've lost my family. Or they lost me.

Either way, for the first time in my life, I'm completely alone.

CHAPTER 2

"God gave us the acorns,
but He doesn't crack them open for us."
—Isaiah

I hear a siren.

Flashes of red light slice through the darkness, along with the shrieks of a siren. Yipes! Someone just sounded the alarm.

I want to hide forever in the darkest corner of this dripping drain, but something inside me says, *Keep running, Isaiah. Never let them catch you! Go find your family! Hurry! Move it or lose it!*

I scamper deeper into the darkness.

I'm extremely speedy. It's all those months I spent on the exercise wheel. Swinging out my tail for balance, I round a blind curve. The strobing flashes of red disappear. So does all the other light. I use my whiskers, just like Mom taught me before she disappeared from the Horrible Place, to feel my way along the damp walls. I barrel headfirst into a black tunnel of nothingness.

And my feet keep getting wetter.

Suddenly, up ahead, I see a split shaft of light.

It's another storm drain.

I scuttle up the slick side wall and come out in an alley littered with trash, some of which looks pretty tasty. But when you're a mouse on the run, trying to catch up with the rest of your family, you really can't stop for a snack, no matter how tempting. I slip on a squishy brown banana peel, slide sideways toward a pile of boxes, and skid through an opening skinnier than a page in a book.

When I glide out (on my bottom) on the other side, I hear voices.

Human voices.

"Find them, you idiot!" snarls one. "Find them all!"

"This isn't my fault," blubbers the other. "I only left the ding-dang door open for a second."

I don't wait to hear any more.

I scale the side of a building. Climb straight up

it using tiny holes that humans wouldn't even know were there. When I reach the top, I see a thick, black utility line swaying in the breeze. I spring off the wall, fly through the air, and land with a *boing* and a bounce.

Using my tail for balance, the way a tightrope walker uses a pole, I race along the bobbing wire.

Soon I'm over another alley. Or maybe a toxic waste dump. The air smells so extremely gross, it makes my whiskers quiver. Rust. Putrid chemicals. The scent of rotting eggs.

My ears are blasted by the shrieks of that alarm horn. It makes my spine shiver all the way down to the tip of my tail. I need my brothers and sisters to buck me up and make me brave.

But I still can't see any of them.

I shout down to the ground anyway.

"You guys? Abe? Winnie? Anybody? *Where are you?*"

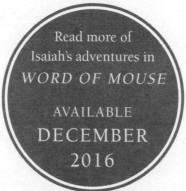

Read more of
Isaiah's adventures in
WORD OF MOUSE

AVAILABLE
DECEMBER
2016

ABOUT THE AUTHORS

JAMES PATTERSON is the internationally best-selling author of the highly praised Middle School books, *Homeroom Diaries*, *Kenny Wright: Superhero*, *Jacky Ha-Ha*, and the I Funny, Treasure Hunters, House of Robots, Maximum Ride, Confessions, Witch & Wizard and Daniel X series. James Patterson has been the most borrowed author in UK libraries for the past nine years in a row and his books have sold more than 325 million copies worldwide, making him one of the biggest-selling authors of all time. He lives in Florida.

CHRIS TEBBETTS has collaborated with James Patterson on five other books in the Middle School series as well as *Kenny Wright: Superhero*. He is also the author of The Viking, a fantasy adventure series for young readers. He lives in Vermont.

JOMIKE TEJIDO is an author-illustrator who has illustrated more than one hundred children's books. He is based in Manila with his wife and his six-year-old daughter, who loves playing with her dog. Oso is a fluffy chow chow who has a cameo appearance on page 84.

Other books in the Middle School series